Abby Walsh was the answer to their problems.

She was warm and nurturing and certainly knew a lot about children. She'd make a terrific mother for his daughter, Kitty, or any other child. All Jack had to do was marry her and his life finally would get back to at least a semblance of normal.

Yeah, that would work. Marry Abby. Solve Kitty's problems. Solve his own problems and get a sexy wife in the bargain. Even if she did irritate him at times, there was no problem with physical attraction. Not on his part, anyway.

Jack didn't think Abby was indifferent to him, either, though he couldn't say whether that was his ego or his instincts talking. It wouldn't hurt to check it out. Subtly, of course. It might even be fun. What a concept.

He'd be so smooth and charming, Abby would never know what hit her!

Dear Reader,

It's the little things that mean so much. In fact, more than once, "little things" have fueled Myrna Temte's Special Edition novels. One of her miniseries evolved from a newspaper article her mother sent her. The idea for her first novel was inspired by something she'd heard a DJ say on her favorite country-western radio station. And Myrna Temte's nineteenth book, *Handprints,* also evolved in an interesting way. A friend received a special Mother's Day present—a picture of her little girl with finger-painted handprints and a sweet poem entitled "Handprints." Once the story was relayed to Myrna, the seed for another romance novel was planted. And the rest, as they say, is history....

There are plenty of special somethings this month. Bestselling author Joan Elliott Pickart delivers *Single with Twins,* the story of a photojournalist who travels the world in search of adventure, only to discover that *family* makes his life complete. In Lisa Jackson's *The McCaffertys: Matt,* the rugged rancher hero feels that law enforcement is no place for a lady—but soon finds himself making a plea for passion....

Don't miss Laurie Paige's *When I See Your Face,* in which a fiercely independent officer is forced to rely on others when she's temporarily blinded in the line of duty. Find out if there will be a *Match Made in Wyoming* in Patricia McLinn's novel, when the hero and heroine find themselves snowbound on a Wyoming ranch! And *The Child She Always Wanted* by Jennifer Mikels tells the touching tale of a baby on the doorstep bringing two people together for a love too great for either to deny.

Asking authors where they get their ideas often proves an impossible question. However, many ideas come from little things that surround us. See what's around you. And if you have an idea for a Special Edition novel, I'd love to hear from you. Enjoy!

Best,
Karen Taylor Richman, Senior Editor

Please address questions and book requests to:
Silhouette Reader Service
U.S.: 3010 Walden Ave., P.O. Box 1325, Buffalo, NY 14269
Canadian: P.O. Box 609, Fort Erie, Ont. L2A 5X3

Handprints

MYRNA TEMTE

SPECIAL EDITION™

Published by Silhouette Books

America's Publisher of Contemporary Romance

Many thanks to the following people for help with research for this book:
Mary Buckham, Teresa Buddington, Brentwood Elementary School;
Alison Colson, ASCW; Kathie Hayes, Chase Middle School; Rachel E. Sterett,
Deputy Prosecuting Attorney; Laurie Summers, M.B.

This book is dedicated to the loving memory of Pepper, my furry little friend,
dear companion and tireless dispenser of unconditional love.
I hope you finally get to catch those evil squirrels in doggy heaven.

 SILHOUETTE BOOKS

ISBN 0-373-24407-X

HANDPRINTS

Copyright © 2001 by Myrna Temte

Visit Silhouette at www.eHarlequin.com

Printed in U.S.A.

Books by Myrna Temte

Silhouette Special Edition

Wendy Wyoming #483
Powder River Reunion #572
The Last Good Man Alive #643
For Pete's Sake #739
Silent Sam's Salvation #745
Heartbreak Hank #751
The Forever Night #816
Room for Annie #861
A Lawman for Kelly #1075
†*Pale Rider* #1124
A Father's Vow #1172
†*Urban Cowboy* #1181
†*Wrangler* #1238
†*The Gal Who Took the West* #1257
†*Wyoming Wildcat* #1287
Seven Months and Counting... #1375
Handprints #1407

*Cowboy Country
†Hearts of Wyoming

Silhouette Books

Montana Mavericks
Sleeping with the Enemy

MYRNA TEMTE

grew up in Montana and attended college in Wyoming, where she met and married her husband. Marriage didn't necessarily mean settling down for the Temtes—they have lived in six different states, including Washington, where they currently reside. Moving so much is difficult, the author says, but it is also wonderful stimulation for a writer.

Though always a "readaholic," Myrna never dreamed of becoming an author. But while spending time at home to care for her first child, she began to seek an outlet from the never-ending duties of housekeeping and child rearing. She started reading romances and soon became hooked, both as a reader and a writer. Now Myrna appreciates the best of all possible worlds—a loving family and a challenging career that lets her set her own hours and turn her imagination loose.

HANDPRINTS

You like a shiny, tidy house,

And sometimes I do, too.

But I have lots of things to learn,

Like tying my own shoes.

I hurry to try this and that,

And often make a mess.

But gee, I always have such fun,

'Cause, Mommy, you're the best.

You always love my pictures,

My mud pies are great art.

So please don't clean these handprints up,

I made them for your heart.

Chapter One

Assistant County Prosecutor Jack Granger parked his dark blue sedan in the visitors' lot at Mountain View Elementary School, muttering, "Why me and why today?" Rubbing the knotted muscles at the back of his neck, he racked his brain for any excuse to leave without seeing his daughter Kitty's teacher. Unfortunately none existed.

It didn't matter that it was 6:10 on a Thursday afternoon, or that he'd had a brutal day at work, or that he had a briefcase stuffed with case files he needed to read before morning. Kitty was his responsibility. When Ms. Walsh requested a conference, he felt obligated to be there.

Again. And again. And again.

Any normal teacher would have given up on him and gone home by now, but Ms. Walsh was hardly normal. She was the most frustrating individual he'd ever met; considering he worked in the criminal justice system, that said something about her. Okay, maybe that was too harsh—but having a rational discussion with her seemed about as likely as finding a completely reformed sex offender.

With Ms. Walsh, everything was about feelings, not facts. Jack would rather be locked up in a cell for an hour with an armed serial killer than have to figure out her thought processes. He wondered if even God knew where that touchy-feely little woman's mind would go next.

To give Ms. Walsh her due, however, Jack admired her dedication to her students. If she said she'd wait until he arrived, she would do exactly that—even on a sunny afternoon in May. Even if she had to wait until midnight.

Resigning himself to another round of aggravation, he straightened his tie and got out of the car. He reached back inside for his suit coat, hesitating while he questioned the need for such formality. On second thought, when it came to dealing with Ms. Walsh, he needed all the formality he could get.

The last time he'd met with her, she'd nearly driven him crazy. With the constant barrage of permission forms, newsletters and requests for money for everything from lunch in the cafeteria to school photos, the paperwork for having one small child in a public school could keep a full-time secretary busy. He did the best he could, but it seemed that he was always missing *some*thing.

And then Ms. Walsh would have to point it out and he'd feel like an idiot. She jumped from topic to topic. Every so often she seemed to have forgotten who she was talking to and used a cheery, enthusiastic voice more suited to a first grader than an adult. Jeez. He wasn't in the mood to deal with her. He didn't know if he could take her *today*.

He thrust his arms into his jacket sleeves as he entered the building and strode down the corridor to Ms. Walsh's classroom. He'd been here enough times to know the way by heart. He paused in the doorway. There she was, sitting behind her desk, using a pencil eraser to flip through a fat stack of papers.

If he hadn't felt so exhausted, he probably would have chuckled. She was barely five feet tall, blond and cute, with her hair pulled back in a long, curly ponytail. He always thought she looked more like a little girl playing school than an adult, but that was only until she opened her mouth. For such a small person, Ms. Walsh had a large personality.

She looked up, stood and gave him a welcoming smile. He just knew she had to be faking. Yet he still found it appealing. And unsettling. Hell, he was losing his mind. Because the truly odd thing was, in spite of everything she did that bugged him to no end, there was a weird, possibly twisted part of him that actually liked this woman.

"Hello, Mr. Granger. Please, come in," she said, waving him into the room. "I'm sorry to call you in on such short notice."

Preferring to keep his contact with her purely professional, Jack squelched an urge to smile in return. Given half a chance, she'd probably start hugging and patting him the way she always did her students. Wishing she wasn't so damn nice, he walked between the first two rows of tiny desks.

At six-foot-three he'd grown used to being taller than most people. But everything in the first-grade

room was built for the convenience of six-year-old
children. He always felt like an awkward giant whenever he had to come to the school.

She nodded at the visitor's chair on the other side
of her desk. "Please, sit down."

He gave the red, battle-scarred plastic chair a du-
bious glance before carefully lowering himself onto
the seat. Ms. Walsh remained standing, and for a moment, she was at eye level with him. He'd never seen
anyone with such dark green eyes before. The color
of jade, they gazed directly into his, and he felt as if
she could see right through him. Putting on his "court
face," he raised his eyebrows, silently demanding that
she get to the point.

She sat on her own chair and laced her fingers together on top of the stack of papers, the expression
in her eyes serious enough to boost his anxiety level.
"Something happened with Kitty today."

A burning sensation of dread invaded Jack's stomach. The last time someone had said that phrase to
him, he'd lost Gina. Kitty was all he had left now.
She was the very best part of his life, and something
had happened to her? No. Oh, please, God, no.

He wanted to lunge to his feet and demand an explanation, but he'd learned the hard way that exces-
sive displays of emotion created problems rather than
solving them. It took every bit of his willpower to
remain seated, ignore the screaming in his head and
unclench his jaw enough to speak. "Is she all right?
What happened? Why didn't you call me sooner?"

Despite his effort to hide it, his voice must have
given his anxiety away. Ms. Walsh raised her hands,
palms out, patting the air in a calming gesture. "It
wasn't that kind of an emergency, Mr. Granger.

Kitty's fine physically. Her emotional state is another matter.''

That was *it?* Ms. Walsh had made his whole world shudder and it was just this touchy-feely emotional crud again? He should have pretended he hadn't received her message and stayed at work. But he was here now, and he knew Ms. Walsh would not let the issue rest until she'd gotten it out of her system. He might as well hear her out.

He leaned back in his chair, stretched his legs out in front of him and crossed one ankle over the other. ''What's wrong with Kitty's emotional state?''

Ms. Walsh raised her chin as if she knew he wasn't going to take her concerns seriously. ''She's still having problems here at school. We've discussed this before.''

Dizzy with relief and irritated at the same time, Jack repeated her standard lecture about his daughter. ''Right. She's too quiet and withdrawn, she doesn't pay attention in class and I need to spend more time with her. I got all of that the last time I was here, and we've done every single thing you've said to do. What happened today?''

''We made Mother's Day gifts.''

Anger roared through him, and he felt a muscle twitch on the side of his jaw. Damn, he should have remembered how close Mother's Day was. But of all the insensitive stunts for a teacher to pull…. ''And you're surprised that caused a problem? For Pete's sake, what did you expect?'' he demanded. ''Her mother is dead.''

Ms. Walsh's cheeks flushed crimson and her eyes glinted with temper, but her voice remained commendably calm. ''I'm aware of that. She's not my only student who's missing a parent. I always provide an alternative activity for children who are in that position, but Kitty *chose* to make the Mother's Day gift."

"She did?"

Ms. Walsh nodded. "She was quite insistent about it, in fact. And then—" an expression of deep sadness flitted across Ms. Walsh's face "—then she tried to give it to *me*."

Shocked by the thought of Kitty doing such a thing in the first place, and with her teacher of all people in the second, Jack sat back in his chair and stared at Ms. Walsh. "Did you accept it?"

"I didn't think that was a good idea," she said. "I told her she could save it for her grandmother or give it to you."

"That's what upset her?"

Ms. Walsh shook her head. "She didn't get upset."

Jack frowned. "You called me in here to tell me that you're upset because Kitty *didn't* get upset?"

Ms. Walsh nodded again.

"Why?" he asked, not at all sure he really wanted to hear the answer. Women had such a bizarre sense of logic sometimes, especially when they talked about emotions. Ms. Walsh rolled her eyes at the ceiling as if *he* were the dimwit, then held out her hands to him in some sort of a plea, the meaning of which eluded him.

Great. Now she'd start waving her hands around like a Shakespearean actor. God, somebody, anybody, *please,* save him from overly dramatic females.

"If Kitty had cried or acted out in some way, I could have comforted her," she said, "or we could have talked about her feelings."

He folded his arms over his chest. "This doesn't make any sense."

"It would if you had a heart," Ms. Walsh grumbled under her breath.

"Excuse me, I didn't hear that." Of course he *had* heard the remark, but he wanted to see if she had the nerve to repeat it.

Exasperation entered her voice, faint but still detectable. "It wasn't important."

Obviously it *was* important to her, but he didn't intend to prolong this conversation one instant longer than necessary. He probably wouldn't understand the mumbo-jumbo, pop-psychology-ridden explanation she would throw at him, anyway. "I still don't see the problem. What, exactly, did Kitty say?"

"She didn't say anything. She just turned away, crumpled up her Mother's Day gift and dropped it into the trash can." Ms. Walsh sighed. "I've never seen a child look so miserable and resigned. Please, Mr. Granger, believe me when I tell you that Kitty needs professional help."

Jack wanted to yell, but forced himself to speak softly. At least *he* knew that emotions belonged under wraps, not cluttering up an important conversation. "Don't start that therapy nonsense again." He thumped his forefinger on the desk for emphasis. "I've told you before, we tried it after her mother died, and it only made things worse for Kitty."

"In what way?"

"In every way." He cast his mind back to the months following Gina's funeral. Night after night, his daughter had cried herself to sleep, only to awaken in the wee hours, screaming with nightmares. Nothing he'd tried had comforted her, and he'd never felt more helpless, more useless in his life. "It just didn't work."

"That doesn't mean it won't now," she said. "Maybe Kitty was too young then or the counselor's personality didn't click with hers. If she needs help—"

Finding it difficult not to leap to his feet and pace, Jack interrupted. "She doesn't. All she needs is more time."

"It's been two years since her mother's death. If Kitty was going to recover on her own, don't you think she would have shown more progress by now?"

"It takes as long as it takes. There's no set time-table for grieving." God knows, it had taken him a long time even to begin to accept Gina's death. It wasn't any surprise to him that it would take Kitty longer.

Ms. Walsh inhaled deeply, and Jack suspected she was counting to ten. Seeing her rein in her emotions certainly was a switch, as was the calm, well-modulated tone she used next. Had someone been coaching her? Perhaps Ms. Walsh had gone to irri-tation-management classes.

"Of course, there isn't," she said, "but sometimes people need a little help with this kind of an adjust-ment. The social worker here does wonderful work with grieving children. I could get Kitty in to see her early next week."

"No."

She blinked, then shot him a startled glance as if she couldn't believe he wasn't going to add a sen-tence of justification she could refute. Too bad. Cre-ating and tolerating uncomfortable silences was part of his job.

"That won't do, Mr. Granger." Her voice gained volume with every word. "It won't do at all. Whatever is going on with Kitty, it's draining the sparkle and life right out of her, and it's taking a serious toll on her schoolwork."

Jack smiled inwardly. Whoever got angry first always lost the argument. "I'm beginning to think that maybe you don't know as much about children as you think you do, Ms. Walsh. I've done everything you've suggested—"

She cut him off with an impatient chop of one hand. "I know you've tried, but it's simply not enough. As it stands now, I can't promote Kitty to second grade unless she develops some concentration and catches up. She's too far behind the other children."

"What?" Dammit, even he had a limit to the amount of aggravation he could take at one sitting. Pushing back his chair, he stood again, straightening to his full height. "You've never said *that* before and the school year's almost over. Why did you wait so long?"

Ms. Walsh rose and tipped her head way back to meet his gaze. The top of her head didn't even reach his shoulder, but if his height advantage bothered her, he couldn't detect it.

"Like you, I've been hoping Kitty would come around," she said. "She's an extremely bright little girl, but she spends most of the day staring off into space and refusing to participate in class activities with the other children. She's not retaining what she does manage to learn from one day to the next, and she needs to stay on task until she finishes her assignments."

"You are *not* going to hold her back," Jack insisted. "I'll go to the principal, the superintendent of public instruction, or the president of the school board if I have to, but you will *not* hold her back."

The look she gave him could have melted granite. "Go right ahead," she said, mimicking his posture and his soft, deadly tone. "They'll tell you that first grade is absolutely vital to her future academic success."

"Give me a break. She's only six years old." He propped his hands on his hips. "What's so important about the first grade that it can ruin the rest of her school career?"

"Oh, nothing much. First grade is only where they learn to read. And do simple arithmetic and a whole lot of other things that Kitty isn't getting."

Ms. Walsh waved one hand in front of her body as if to encompass the entire room. "It may not seem like much to you, but for the next eleven years everything she studies will build on what she's supposed to learn here. If she doesn't conquer the basics now, she'll struggle through every class she ever takes. Is that what you want for her?"

For a long, excruciating moment, he remained silent, feeling ashamed of himself for taking a cheap shot at a woman who, even though she annoyed the devil out of him, obviously cared a great deal about his daughter. "Of course I don't want that."

Jack felt a knot of fire in the center of his chest. He stepped away from the visitor's chair, wanting to leave and regroup before he said something he'd regret. "I'll have to take this under advisement." He pushed back his cuff and glanced at his watch. "I need to be home in fifteen minutes. I'll let you know what I decide.''

''Hold it right there!'' She scrambled out from behind her desk as if she had some notion of blocking his path. ''We're not finished. I need a better answer than that.''

''I said,'' he said through gritted teeth, ''I'll get back to you.''

She narrowed her eyes and stuck out her chin. ''When?''

''Will next week be soon enough for you?'' He turned and started for the doorway.

''No, it will not.'' She hurried after him. ''None of this is for me, Mr. Granger. It's for Kitty. Can't you see that your child is suffering? And you're just letting it go on and on. She deserves better from you than you're giving her.''

Literally seeing red at her accusations, he came to an abrupt halt and turned back around to face her. ''Do you have any children, Ms. Walsh?''

She paled, and for the first time, her gaze failed to meet his. ''No, I don't.''

He laughed, but it wasn't a pleasant sound, even to his own ears. ''Why am I not surprised? It's always easy to criticize what you don't understand, isn't it.''

''I didn't mean to insult you.'' She reached out, as if she would touch his arm. He stepped back out of range and waited until she lowered her hand to her side.

''Well, you did. And let me tell you, being a parent is a lot harder than it looks to people who've never tried it. Before you start throwing around remarks like that, maybe you should get married and try having a kid of your own.''

Ignoring her horrified expression, he strode out of the room and down the hallway, and slammed through the school's front doors. He desperately wanted to get in his car and drive as fast and as far away from this school, Ms. Walsh and all of Spokane, Washington, as possible, and never come back. But he couldn't give up and run away.

Though he might be a miserable failure as a father, he was all Kitty had. And he was going to do right by her—whatever that meant.

Shading her eyes against the bright sunshine during recess the next morning, Abby Walsh watched Kitty Granger and felt an immediate, all-too-familiar tug at her heart. The little girl sat on the concrete step with her back against the school building, her skinny legs hugged tightly to her chest, her chin resting on her knees, lost in some lonely world only she could see.

Turning to her best friend, Erin Johnson, Abby asked, "Is it just me, or is that kid in serious trouble?"

Erin snorted, then stared at Abby in obvious disbelief. "Well, duh. That's hardly normal behavior for a six-year-old."

Abby allowed herself to relax a smidgeon. A child psychologist with a thriving practice, Erin always called things exactly the way she saw them. If Erin saw a problem, there must be one. Still, Abby couldn't stop herself from asking for more reassurance. "You're *positive* it's not just me?"

"Your instincts are usually right on target when it comes to kids. Why doubt yourself now?"

"You've never met Kitty's daddy, Granger the Grump." Abby glanced back toward the playground,

automatically counting heads. First graders were so
unpredictable when they went outside, a teacher
couldn't be too careful about keeping track of them.
"When I've talked to him about getting her into
counseling, he's always convinced me I was overre-
acting. I needed an expert opinion to be sure I wasn't
imagining anything."

Erin inclined her head toward Kitty. "She should
be playing, but she's just sitting there all by herself.
She's not even watching the other kids, and she looks
so sad, I can't believe she's not crying."

"Do you think she's clinically depressed?"

"It's impossible to be sure without talking to her,
which we both know I can't do without her father's
permission," Erin said with a grimace.

Abby gave Erin's forearm a squeeze. "Just give
me your best professional guess."

"My best professional guess is that the poor child
is depressed and probably has been since her mother
died," Erin replied. "She's showing classic symptoms, and God knows she's got a good reason to be
depressed. At the very least, she needs an assessment."

"Thanks." Abby breathed a soft sigh of relief to
have her own perceptions verified. "How do I convince her hardheaded father to change his mind about
counseling?"

Erin shot her a wry smile. "Remember he's a prosecutor, which means he's probably a just-the-facts
kind of a guy. Don't get emotional when you talk to
him or he'll turn you off."

Abby rolled her eyes toward heaven, then admitted,
"Well, it's already too late for that. I think his face
would crack if he actually smiled. Every time I call

him in for a conference, he acts like I'm imposing on his precious time. I'm telling you, he's a royal pain in the—''

''This isn't about you or grumpy Mr. Granger,'' Erin interrupted. ''It's about a little girl who needs help.''

Wincing, Abby pretended to look behind Erin. ''Where do you keep it?''

''Keep what?''

''That guilt cannon you just fired at me.''

Erin chuckled. ''Hit the target, did I?''

''Dead center,'' Abby confessed. ''And you're right. It's about Kitty.''

''What happened with him yesterday?''

Abby shrugged, then looked away. ''I lost my temper and sort of let my mouth run away without my brain.''

''You've got to stop doing that, Ab. How bad was it?''

Abby replayed the conversation, editing out his parting shot. Erin remained quiet, clearly allowing Abby's words to echo in her mind.

Abby sighed when the silence stretched out, then finally said, ''I really blew it, didn't I.''

''What are you going to do about it?''

''What *can* I do?''

''He might appreciate an apology.''

''Well, so would I.'' Abby bit off an indignant huff. ''I could have handled it better, but he wasn't exactly Mr. Nice Guy, either.''

''Abby,'' Erin chided. ''What are you going to do for Kitty's sake?''

''Well, I could write him a note tonight, and he'll get it on Monday.''

"Why wait until Monday?" Erin said in a calm, infuriating manner. "That gives him a whole weekend to build up his defenses, and it's exactly what a man like your grump would expect."

"He's not *my* grump," Abby protested. "He's not *my* anything, thank heaven. Where are you going with this?"

Erin fell silent for a moment, then said, "Do something he won't expect. Push *him* off balance for once."

"I'd rather push him off a cliff." When Erin simply stared at her in response, Abby gave in. "All right, it's hard to imagine him off balance, but I'll bite. What won't he expect?"

"You've always met with him at school," Erin said. "Why don't you invade his turf for a change?"

"What?" Abby yelped, appalled at the idea.

"It's perfect. Show up at his house tonight with an apology and a plate of cookies as a peace offering."

"He'll throw me off his property."

"Mr. Dignified, Public Servant Granger?" Erin laughed. "He will not. He'll have to be gracious, and you'll get a chance to see what he and Kitty are like at home. You can collect a lot of information from a home visit."

"And you'd be happy to interpret that information for me."

"Absolutely," Erin agreed. "Are you willing to try it?"

Abby considered the question, wondering where she would find the courage to deal with Granger the Grump twice in one week.

"All right, I'll do it. And this time, I'll be absolutely logical and businesslike, if it kills me."

Abby glanced at Kitty again. She was a beautiful child with fine, shiny black hair no ponytail holder could contain for long, sad brown eyes, an adorable little nose and a sweet bow mouth that rarely smiled. "She's the sweetest little girl in the world, and I can't stand seeing her look so lost and alone all the time."

"She's *his* daughter, Ab."

Abby stiffened. "I'm not likely to forget *that*. But what kind of a father can't see what's happening to his own child?"

"Don't be so judgmental," Erin scolded her. "He's probably struggling to get through one day at a time, like most other single parents. He still may be suffering with his own grief. Or he may be in denial. None of which makes him a bad father."

Sniffing, Abby crossed her arms over her breasts. "Well, there is no way I'm going to back off and let him ruin that child."

Erin pinned her with a stare. "I thought you weren't going to get involved with your students anymore."

"I'm not."

"Then who was that warrior-woman I just heard? Mighty defender of the girl-child and all that?"

Abby turned her head away. "You imagined her."

"If it looks like a duck and it quacks like a duck..." Erin uttered a wry laugh. "I think maybe we should reconsider the idea of your going to his house."

"Don't be such a worrywart." Abby smiled and squeezed Erin's arm again. "I'm just going to convince Mr. Granger to hire you as Kitty's therapist. You'll take wonderful care of her, and I'll be able to leave Spokane knowing she's going to be all right."

"And you'll stop at recommending me? You promise you won't get any more involved with the Grangers than that?"

"It depends on Mr. Granger and Kitty."

Erin shot her a worried look. "Abby—"

Abby let out an exasperated huff. "Trust me, there's no danger of starting a personal relationship that could become a problem later. I'm a professional. I know what I'm doing."

Chapter Two

Can't you see that your child is suffering?

"No, she's not," Jack muttered as he drove home on Friday night. He knew about suffering from first-hand experience. Kitty had suffered the most when she'd been in therapy before, dammit, but Ms. Walsh didn't understand that. Or maybe she just didn't want to believe it.

Wishing he could strangle someone, he tightened his fingers around the steering wheel until his knuckles hurt. He'd gone over his meeting with Ms. Walsh in his mind a hundred times since yesterday, but her words continued to haunt him.

And you're just letting it go on and on.

"Oh, you're so damn smug," he said. "You weren't there. You don't know what she went through."

She deserves better from you than you're giving her.

"Yeah, well, so what else is new? I'm doing the best I can, but it'll never be enough. It'll never be as good as what Gina could've done for her, either. And there's not much I can do about that, is there?"

He crossed the Little Spokane River and pulled into his long, gravel driveway, a sense of inadequacy chomping at his insides in spite of all his muttering. Parking beside the 1940s farmhouse he and Gina had started to remodel, he got out of the car and stood there for a moment, waiting for the inevitable pang of loss and loneliness to ease. God, he still missed her, for his own sake as well as his daughter's.

Gina had been more than a wife to him. She'd been his soul mate. They'd been high school sweethearts, they'd given their virginity to each other. He'd never been with another woman, had never wanted anyone else.

He knew it was time now to move on. Knew that Gina wouldn't want or expect him to spend the rest of his life alone. But it was hard.

He told himself to stop wallowing in his grief and think about something else. Surveying his property, he grimaced at what he saw. There was still so much to be done. But between his job and taking care of Kitty, he never had any time to *start* a home-improvement project, much less finish one.

The back door banged open and Millie Patten, his housekeeper and baby-sitter, stepped out onto the stoop, propping her hands on her ample hips. Jack took one look at her disappointed expression and bit back a curse. Great. Just what he needed—another dose of guilt.

Millie was a sweet, hardworking woman. She reminded him of a grandmother or a great-aunt who loves you without reservation, but at the same time feels compelled to "help" you correct all your major and minor faults. It was all done with the best of intentions and in the most loving possible way, of course. Loving, like a defense lawyer on a crusade.

"Oh, Jack." she said, drawing out each syllable in a soft tone that made him feel ten times worse than a scolding one would have. "Do you have any idea what time it is, dear?"

Sometimes the woman drove him nuts with her unsolicited advice, but her job had been damn hard to fill. Unlike too many of her predecessors, she was competent and reliable, and she dearly loved Kitty. That was all that really mattered.

"Sorry, Millie," he said. "I'll do better next week."

"That's what you always say," she replied. "But you're still late nearly every night, and it isn't right."

"Well, at least I'm good for the overtime."

She sadly shook her head at him. "That's not the point, dear. You need to spend more time with Kitty. And you need to stop burying yourself in work and get a social life of your own."

Jack approached her, the fingers of his left hand locked around the handle of his briefcase in a punishing grip. "If I had a social life, I wouldn't be able to spend as much time with Kitty as I do now."

"At least you'd have some hope of finding her a mother."

"Millie, please. I appreciate your concern, but you'll just have to let *me* worry about that. All right?"

She turned on the run-down heel of the athletic

shoes she always wore and marched back into the house. Jack followed her inside, calculated what he owed her for the week and handed her a check. "I'll see you Monday morning."

"All right. But do try to play with Kitty this weekend. She needs your attention."

He shut the door behind her and jabbed one hand through his hair in frustration. Jeez. Did she really think he intended to ignore his daughter all weekend? Loosening his tie with one hand, he flipped through the stack of mail, then carried the bills and his briefcase into the den.

The massive desk and the files he'd brought home called to him, enticing him to escape from the upheaval in his personal life to the sanctuary of work. Compared to the constant ambiguity of raising a child, the law was blessedly clear.

The sound of the television drifted into the den from the family room. Draping his coat and tie over the back of his chair, he went to find Kitty, rolling up his shirtsleeves on the way. As expected, she was curled up on the overstuffed sofa, staring at the TV as if entranced.

Jack crossed the room. Kitty looked up at him with Gina's brown eyes, but didn't speak. Her eyes were huge in her small, pale face, and her ponytail holder had slipped over to one side of her head. There must be a trick to putting those things in so they'd stay put, but he hadn't yet found it.

"Hi, Kitten," he said. "What are you up to?"

Kitty shrugged one shoulder, then inclined her head toward the television. "Watching kid shows."

He glanced at the TV. A weird-looking creature with blue fur and googly eyes cavorted across the screen with a group of children. "So I see. Is this a good one?"

She shrugged the same shoulder. He searched for another topic, but drew a blank. How this could happen to him, he didn't know. Every day he talked to all kinds of people, from defendants and their attorneys, to cops and judges, to crime victims and their families, but he couldn't even make decent chitchat with his own daughter.

"Are you hungry?" he asked.

Wrinkling her nose, Kitty shook her head. "Not very."

He checked his watch. "It's past your dinnertime."

Kitty bounced her left leg against the sofa in a quick, rhythmic pattern. "Can't help it, Daddy. I'm just not hungry."

"Did you have a snack after school?"

"Uh-uh. Didn't want one."

Studying her with a more critical eye, Jack frowned. Her face was painfully thin. So were her arms and legs. Had she lost weight or just grown? He wasn't sure, but he knew she looked too scrawny to be healthy. When had *that* happened? He could have sworn she'd looked fine when he'd driven her to school that morning. Frustrated that he hadn't noticed the change in her appearance sooner, he held out a hand to her.

"Well, I'm starving. Come and set the table for me. Maybe that'll help you work up an appetite."

Kitty slowly sat up. Then, with obvious reluctance, she pushed herself to her feet, but made no move to take his hand. Assuming she would follow, Jack walked back to the kitchen.

This was the one completely renovated room in the

whole house, and though he was an indifferent cook, he appreciated the modern, efficient layout Gina had created. He washed his hands at the faucet, then pulled a step stool up to the sink for Kitty while he rummaged through the pantry and the refrigerator.

Ugh. He didn't feel like cooking. A burger or a taco or a pizza sounded great, but he'd been studying nutrition lately—at Millie's urging. Kitty needed fresh, healthy food, not an overdose of salt and saturated fat. He pulled out the green salad Millie had made, a package of chicken breasts, fresh broccoli and potatoes for the microwave.

Kitty set the table, dragging herself back and forth between the table and the cupboards. Watching her covertly, Jack felt increasingly alarmed. In one of his child-rearing books he'd read that six-year-old kids were supposed to run around and drive their parents crazy with about a thousand questions a day. So why wasn't Kitty doing that?

Dammit, he'd worked so hard to learn how to be a good parent. And now, because of Ms. Busybody Walsh, he was seeing problems everywhere he looked.

But what if Kitty really *was* suffering, and he wasn't seeing it because he didn't *want* to see it? Was that even possible?

He hated the familiar worry clamoring for his attention, dreaded the sleepless nights he knew would follow. Thank you, Ms. Walsh. Why couldn't that woman mind her own damn business?

At seven-thirty Abby climbed into her red Bronco, drove north on Division Street and made her way to Little Spokane River Drive where the Grangers lived.

The sun was almost to the western horizon, filling the sky with a soft, reddish glow. The air was cool and sweet, the scenery pretty as the road cut through alternating sections of productive farmland and new residential developments.

There were some big, beautiful homes out here, but she wondered how a public official like Mr. Granger could afford the steep prices the area demanded. Maybe he'd inherited a lot of money, or his wife had carried a hefty life insurance policy. Or maybe his family had owned one of the original homesteads.

It was none of her business, of course, but a healthy dose of curiosity rarely hurt anyone, and it made life much more interesting. The two-lane road followed the dips and rises of the spring-green foothills and the sparkling curves of the river. Abby rolled down the window, drinking in the soft, country sounds of birds and the rich, earthy smells of farm animals and freshly plowed fields.

Two miles later she spotted a barn-shaped mailbox painted with the distinctive black-and-white spots of a Holstein cow. Wrought-iron numbers bearing the Grangers' address stretched across the top. She crossed the small bridge and drove down a long, gravel driveway into the farmyard. Turning off the engine, she sat behind the steering wheel and studied the property with interest.

She had expected an imposing, immaculate house and perfectly manicured grounds judging from Mr. Granger's impeccable appearance and rigid personality. But while the white, two-story clapboard house was certainly imposing, its barren front porch and empty flower beds gave it a sad aura that reminded her of Kitty. Despite its neglected appearance, however, it had great potential to look homey and inviting.

If it were hers, she would spend the summer decorating that big front porch with wind chimes and wicker furniture with bright, even gaudy cushions, and filling those flower beds with color and life.

Abby slung her school satchel over her shoulder, then grabbed the plastic-wrapped plate of chocolate chip cookies and climbed out of the Bronco. Her stomach tightened with apprehension, but she straightened her spine and set off across the yard. Bracing herself for unpleasantness, she knocked on the door.

Seconds later she heard footsteps, the door swung inward and Granger the Grouch stood in the opening. On a purely physical basis, she found Jack Granger extremely attractive. His features were rugged enough to make his face really interesting. Though they were usually cold and distant, his blue eyes revealed a fierce intelligence that fascinated her.

She preferred men who weren't quite so big, but she had to admit she'd admired his broad shoulders, narrow waist and long limbs more than once. Even a suit and tie couldn't hide such a fit, well-defined physique.

His evening beard had sprouted. He still wore his suit pants, but the coat and tie were missing and his white shirt hung open at the neck. All the way down to the third button. The *V* of chest exposed was tanned and matted with crisp dark hair. Oh, goodness, that slightly rumpled look *was* an improvement.

"You," he said, leaving no doubt whatsoever that finding her on his porch was anything but a nice surprise.

She smiled at him. "Hello, Mr. Granger."

"What are you doing here?"

Abby cleared her throat and forced herself to meet his angry gaze. Uh-oh. She pulled herself up to her full height, imagined herself taller. Much, much taller. None of it eased the tension crackling between them. She shoved the cookies toward his midsection. He grabbed for the plate, fumbled with it when she yanked her hand away too quickly, but saved it before it hit the floor.

"I brought a peace offering," she said, while he was still juggling the plate. "I want to apologize for yesterday. I'm just…" She paused, groping for exactly the right words to express herself in a way he would not only understand, but accept. "I look at Kitty and she's such a sweet little girl and I see so much potential in her, I'm extremely frustrated to see her floundering."

"And you think I'm not?"

Abby held her palms in front of her shoulders, hoping that small gesture could soothe his irritation. "Of course you are. I didn't mean to imply otherwise. I think there's another avenue to explore in order to help Kitty, but I know you're a caring father who's doing his best in what must be a very difficult situation. I let my frustration and temper get the better of me, and I really am sorry for the way I spoke to you."

The stiffness in his posture eased fractionally, and his voice lost its hard edge. "I appreciate your apology."

She reached into the satchel, pulled out the sheaf of papers she'd brought along and handed them to him. This time she didn't have to force a smile. He didn't return it, but he studied her mouth as if he realized there was something new or different he should notice. Her lips tingled.

"This is a copy of our school district's learning targets for first grade," she said, pretending not to see the way he startled at the sound of her voice. "It lists everything Kitty should be able to do in order to move on to second grade."

He set the cookies on something inside, then leafed through the first five sheets, his eyes opening wider with each page before he looked at her again. "All of this?"

Abby nodded. "And that's just the district's requirements. We also have EARLS, or Essential Academic Learning Requirements, and Benchmarks from the State Board of Education."

"May I study this?" he asked.

"Keep it. I can always print another one off the district's Web site. I thought it would give you a more realistic idea of how much Kitty still needs to learn before I can promote her."

"I see."

"Ms. Walsh?"

Abby glanced down and discovered a wide-eyed Kitty standing beside her father. The little girl wore the same pink shorts outfit she'd had on at school, and she was gazing up at Abby with a tentative grin that made Abby's arms ache to hug her.

"Did you come to visit me?" Kitty asked.

Abby automatically crouched down until she was at eye level with the little girl. "I brought your daddy some papers and some cookies, too."

"Really?" Kitty said.

"Yes, ma'am," Abby replied. "They'll taste great with some milk."

"Are you gonna eat them with me?"

Seeing more animation in the little girl's face than she had in weeks, Abby hesitated. She would love to accept the invitation to gather information for Erin, as well as for Kitty's sake, but Mr. Granger's warning scowl squelched that idea. She didn't want to push her luck too far, after all. "I'm sorry, sweetie, but I shouldn't."

Kitty craned her neck to look up at her father. "Ask her to stay, Daddy."

"Ms. Walsh already said she can't," he said, his tone calm and quiet.

Kitty raised her chin to an uncommonly stubborn angle; Abby had rarely seen her care about anything enough to make a fuss. "But she'll stay if *you* ask her. I know she will."

Clearly surprised and not a little dismayed by his daughter's argument, it was Mr. Granger's turn to hesitate. While he obviously didn't want to invite her into his house, he just as obviously didn't want to disappoint Kitty, either. He looked so torn, Abby almost laughed.

"Well, Ms. Walsh?" he finally said, his voice little more than a grumble. "Would you like to come in for cookies?"

Abby couldn't help chuckling at his grudging invitation. "Hey, when you put it that way, I'm never too busy to have a cookie with one of my favorite students."

Kitty raised her head and gaped at Abby. The smile of sheer delight that immediately spread across the little girl's face made the whole trip out here worth it, as far as Abby was concerned. Kitty dashed forward, took Abby's hand and tugged her toward the threshold.

Abby took a couple of steps, halting when she realized Mr. Granger hadn't moved. He looked huge, disgruntled and about as movable as a boulder. With his broad shoulders and his feet spread wide apart, he filled up most of the doorway. She wondered if he was having second thoughts about inviting her in. Or maybe he was using his size in an attempt to intimidate her, reminding her of who was in charge here.

She was ashamed to admit, even to herself, that it was working. It annoyed her to no end because she usually paid little attention to anyone else's size in relation to her own. To her mind, she wasn't overly short; other people were overly tall. But whenever she had to talk to Mr. Granger, she always felt like a Chihuahua yapping at a Great Dane.

Too bad for him, she'd die before he would ever see it.

Plastering a smile on her lips, she turned sideways and followed Kitty inside. Though she tightened her muscles when she passed him, her breasts still brushed against his abdomen. He felt as hard and solid as that boulder she'd imagined. It had been so long since she'd had even this much contact with a man's body, the instant shock of sexual awareness froze her in place.

His harshly drawn breath drew her gaze to his. To her amazement, she saw that same shocked awareness she was experiencing reflected in his eyes. He immediately stepped back, leaving enough space for a shopping cart to pass through without touching either of them. His gaze remained locked with hers, however, and she found it impossible to break eye contact.

Finally, Kitty gave her hand an impatient jerk, pulling Abby through the doorway and breaking the spell. Feeling an unfortunate urge to laugh hysterically, Abby grabbed the plate of cookies from an entryway table and allowed the little girl to lead her away.

They walked through a formal living room. It was furnished with classic, conservative pieces of furniture covered in earth-toned, practical fabrics that suited the Grump's personality, but horrified Abby. Good heavens, it all blended as beautifully as a magazine layout, but the whole room desperately needed more light and color, and it was painfully neat. Far too neat for a sane adult, much less anyone raising a young child.

Didn't this kid own any toys?

The kitchen was more of the same cool perfection, though it clearly had been designed with a woman's convenience in mind. It was impossible to imagine making enough of a mess in this room to cook anything that didn't come in a microwavable package. Abby blinked, then shivered.

"Come on, Ms. Walsh." Releasing Abby's hand, Kitty ran across the kitchen, dragged a step stool over to the refrigerator and opened the door. "I'll get the milk."

Abby quickly deposited the cookies on the table and hurried to Kitty's side to lend her a hand if she needed one. When Mr. Granger entered the room, she ignored him. He walked to one of the cupboards, took out three small plates and three glasses, and carried them to the table, his movements brisk and efficient.

She didn't catch a whiff of his subtle aftershave, notice he looked tired or feel one bit distracted because he still hadn't fastened those three buttons on his shirt. She didn't even see that tanned slice of bare chest playing peek-a-boo as he moved around the room. No, siree. What a liar she was.

Annoyed by her adolescent, inappropriate reactions to him, Abby said, ''I'm afraid those glasses won't do, Mr. Granger.''

He shot her an incredulous look, as if he couldn't believe she had the nerve to question his judgment. Well, too bad. It was his own fault for distracting her.

''What's wrong with them?'' he asked.

''They're too tall.''

''Too tall for what?''

''For dunking cookies, of course,'' Abby replied. ''Shorter cups work much better.''

''We don't dunk cookies at our house,'' he said flatly.

''Mommy used to let me sometimes,'' Kitty said, her voice so soft that it was barely audible. Setting the milk carton on the table, she climbed onto one of the straight-backed wooden chairs, twisted her fingers together in her lap and looked at them. ''She said I should only do it at home, but cookies taste better that way.''

Mr. Granger stared at her. After a moment, he swallowed, then abruptly returned to the cupboards, put the glasses away and brought three mugs back to the table.

Having glimpsed real pain in his eyes, Abby set out to give him a moment to collect himself. She stripped the plastic wrap off the paper plate and offered it to the little girl. ''Well, now, Miss Kitty, would you care to try one of these super-duper chocolate chip numbers?''

"Yes, please." She carefully selected a cookie and placed it neatly in the center of her plate.

Abby winced inside. Erin had been right about how much a person could learn about a family from an in-home visit. No six-year-old child should be this perfect. Making a tsking sound, she sadly shook her head.

"Oh, that poor little cookie looks so lonely sitting there all by itself. I think you'd better take another one to keep it company."

Kitty gave her a shy grin, then looked to her father for permission. Nodding, he gently touched her hair. "Go ahead, Kitten. No telling what a lonely cookie might do."

Swallowing at a lump that had suddenly invaded her own throat, Abby held the plate until Kitty selected another cookie. Jeez, it wasn't fair for the Grump to call his daughter Kitten and stroke her hair as if she were the most fragile, precious thing in his world. If he kept that up, Abby might actually have to start liking him, which would only confuse the heck out of her.

Abby served herself a cookie and sat down beside Kitty. Mr. Granger filled the cups and sat on the opposite side of the table. He selected a cookie for himself, then looked directly at Abby, his expression clearly saying, *All right. What next?*

Abby smiled, more than happy to accept his silent challenge. Maintaining eye contact, she dunked a cookie halfway into her cup, let it soak up the cold milk and quickly stuffed it into her mouth, closing her eyes and making noises of ecstasy as the flavors hit her taste buds.

"Mmm, mmm, mmm."

Giggling, Kitty followed her example.

Mr. Granger watched them both with a wry smile. When he finally began to eat his own cookie, he didn't join in with the dunking fun, but he didn't say anything to discourage Kitty's fun, either. Abby would have given a great deal to know what he was thinking, but she focused her attention where it belonged—on Kitty.

Kitty took forever to finish her snack, but at last she wiped her mouth with the back of her hand, which, in Abby's opinion, was more appropriate for a little girl than the paper napkin her father had given her.

With shining eyes, Kitty turned to Abby. "Would you like to see my bedroom, Ms. Walsh?"

"We've already taken up enough of Ms. Walsh's time," Mr. Granger said.

The little girl shot her father a rebellious scowl and crossed her arms over her chest. "But I want Ms. Walsh to see my room."

"It's almost your bedtime, Kitten. Go upstairs and get ready, and I'll be up to read to you in a few minutes."

Kitty looked to Abby, obviously hoping that she would overrule her father, but Abby suddenly saw a bone-deep weariness in his eyes and slowly shook her head. "Your daddy's right. I do need to get home. I'll see you on Monday, okay?"

Abby held her breath, hoping that Kitty would argue for what she wanted, and for a moment, the little girl looked as if she just might do it. But then her eyes stopped shining, her shoulders slumped, and she murmured, "Okay, Ms. Walsh. Thank you for the cookies."

"You're welcome, honey. I'm glad you liked them."

Picking up her plate and mug, Kitty carried them to the sink and left the room. The poor little scrap looked so much like a deflated balloon, Abby had to blink back tears. The tension in the kitchen grew to painful proportions while they studied each other across the table, waiting for Kitty to get out of earshot. Finally, the sound of running water filtered down from upstairs.

"Thank you," he said quietly.

"For what?"

"For staying. It meant a lot to Kitty."

"I wanted her to know she's important to me," Abby said. "And I didn't want her to worry that I was upset with her because I turned down her Mother's Day gift."

"I appreciate that. She obviously likes you."

He didn't *say* that he didn't like her, but the implication was there in the air between them. Yet he seemed more open to a discussion about Kitty now than he had earlier. Abby took a deep breath, then plunged right in.

"Look, Mr. Granger, we're supposed to be on the same side, here. Don't you think we can find a way to work together to help Kitty?"

"You'd think so." He rubbed the back of his neck with one hand, then reached for another cookie. "We don't seem to agree on much, though."

"We don't have to." Abby tilted her head to one side, shaking it when he offered her the cookie plate. "I thought the way Kitty acted tonight was promising."

"In what way?"

"It was refreshing to see her act so much like a regular kid tonight."

"Well, she *is* a regular kid."

Abby gaped at him. "How can you say that after seeing what just happened to her?"

"Nothing happened to her. What are you talking about?"

"She was giggly and lively for a while. She used to be that way all the time, didn't she?"

Impatience—or perhaps it was defensiveness—sharpened his voice. "What's your point?"

"Tonight I saw the little girl I'll bet Kitty used to be. She needs to become that little girl again if she's going to have a happy life. She should be animated and obnoxious and argue for what she wants like any other kid, instead of being that overly polite, sad little ghost who just left the room."

"You're exaggerating."

"I'm not. You sat right there and saw it yourself. When you refused to let me see her room, all of that life and fun drained right out of her."

"Are you saying that I should never say no to her?"

"Of course not. But would it really have hurt—"

"Ms. Walsh," he interrupted. "We're not going to get anywhere with this tonight, so you'll have to excuse me. Thank you for your concern, but I need to go and take care of my daughter."

"Fine." Abby carried her plate and mug to the sink and set them beside Kitty's.

Mr. Granger escorted her to the front door and held it open for her. Unable to resist, she pointed at the stack of papers he'd left sitting on the entry table. "Do study those learning targets, and you'll see how much farther Kitty needs to go. If you change your mind about getting her into counseling, let me know. I have several excellent people I can recommend.''

''Good *night,* Ms. Walsh.''

''Good night, Mr. Granger.''

She hurried down the steps, climbed into her Bronco and turned the key in the ignition, pausing a moment to take one last look at the Grangers' house. Mr. Granger had already gone inside and shut the front door. There were lights on in one of the upstairs rooms, and, looking at the window, Abby could make out the shape of Kitty's head. A little hand came up and waved at her.

Abby waved back. She still had three full weeks of school left. In that amount of time, she'd find a way to help Kitty, whether Mr. Granger liked it or not. And while she was at it, she was going to help him, too.

He'd always seemed so strong and sure of himself, she'd never actually thought of him as someone in pain. Though he obviously was in deep denial where Kitty was concerned, Abby believed there was hope for him yet. She didn't doubt for a second that once he saw for himself what Kitty needed, he would move heaven and earth to get it for her. Now all Abby had to do was find a way to get him to see his daughter in a more realistic light.

She was going to have to behave herself, though. She couldn't afford to fool herself about the attraction she felt for both the Grangers, but especially for Jack. A true professional wouldn't have even noticed how sexy he could be when he wasn't acting like a grump-face.

Chapter Three

Three hours later, Jack sat at his desk, plowing through the files he'd brought home. He needed concentration to commit the important facts of each case to memory, but tonight it wasn't there. He tossed down his pen in frustration, then heard a low cry coming from upstairs.

He took the stairs three at a time, entered Kitty's room and stood watching her. She'd kicked off her covers, her hair was plastered to her forehead with perspiration and parallel tear trails glistened on her flushed cheeks. Her head thrashing back and forth, she repeatedly whimpered the one word guaranteed to rip his heart right down the middle.

"Mommyyyy."

Kitty had cried in her sleep every night for five months after Gina's death. The memories of that time still had the power to bring him to his knees. Lord, he couldn't stand it if she started doing this again. He picked up Kitty and cuddled her against his chest, stroking her hair.

"Shh, Kitten," he crooned. "It's all right. I'm here."

"Mommy."

"I know, baby. I know. I miss her, too."

Shivering, she heaved a huge, wobbly sigh, rested her cheek against his shoulder, then snuggled closer. He kissed the top of her head, rubbing her back and rocking her. When she relaxed into that boneless state only children achieve, he lay her in the middle of her bed and pulled the covers over her.

He stood there, anxiously watching. It didn't take a genius to figure out what had brought this on. He'd like to strangle that pint-size buttinsky teacher and her blasted Mother's Day project for stirring up memories and emotions that were better left alone. Kitty shouldn't have to suffer one more second of pain over her mother's death.

Ms. Walsh could just butt right back out of their lives, because Kitty was all right, dammit. And he would prove it to that little woman. The best way to do that was to get Kitty caught up with the rest of her classmates.

Hurrying downstairs, he found the stack of papers Ms. Walsh had delivered, took them into the den and settled in behind his desk. Good grief, there were learning targets for reading and math, for writing, social studies, physical education, music and art, even behavior. It seemed like an awful lot of things for such little kids to have to learn in one school year.

He flipped back to the math section. "Recognizes and writes numerals from 1 to 100," he read. "Counts sets of objects less than 100 using a variety of grouping strategies such as twos, fives and tens. Verbalizes and records addition and subtraction problems.''

The list went on. Trying to guess how many of those things Kitty could do gave him a hollow feeling in the middle of his chest. Could she do any of them? Not enough. Well, damn. They'd have to work on this stuff, of course, but what if she really couldn't retain the things she learned? What if she truly was depressed?

No, that was ridiculous. Kitty wasn't depressed. He would know if she was in serious trouble. Of course, he would.

Slowly and much more carefully, he reread the papers, going all the way to the bottom of the stack. The last page was the infamous Mother's Day gift. At least, he thought that was what it must be. He held it up with both hands.

The single, wrinkled page had a recent photo of Kitty, a set of her handprints done in bright red paint and a poem.

HANDPRINTS

You like a shiny, tidy house,
And sometimes I do too.
But I have lots of things to learn,
Like tying my own shoes.
I hurry to try this and that,
And often make a mess.
But gee, I always have such fun,
'Cause, Mommy, you're the best.
You always love my pictures,
My mud pies are great art.
So please don't clean these handprints up,
I made them for your heart.

Jack cleared his tight throat and rubbed one hand down over his face, wiping a trace of dampness from his eyes. Damn. The photo, the handprints and the poem were all so sweet and sentimental, Gina would have cried buckets over them. He set the paper on the desk and pushed it to one side.

Kitty had wanted to give it to Ms. Walsh. If Ms. Walsh had accepted it, he never would have seen it. Suddenly he felt as if he didn't even know his own daughter anymore. He could understand that she might need to have a female role model, but of all the women in the world for Kitty to latch on to, Ms. Walsh would be dead last on his list. She was too emotional. Too bossy. Too...well, just too convinced she was right about everything.

Oh, yeah? And who would be first on your list?

He wanted to tell that mocking inner voice to shut up, but he knew from experience that it wouldn't leave him alone until he answered the damn question. So, who would be first on his list? There was always his mother. Unfortunately, she lived in Texas, and Kitty only saw her for about a week once a year. It was the same story with Gina's mother, who lived in New York City.

Since his two brothers were still bachelors and Gina had been an only child, there were no doting aunts for Kitty. He didn't mix his private life with his professional one, which let out his co-workers. There were no girlfriends; he wasn't even interested in dating yet.

Who did that leave? Millie Patten? Well, Millie had her good points, but she was a little old for Kitty to identify with and she could be awfully pushy sometimes.

All right, so now Kitty's attachment to the teacher made more sense. When he'd seen her at work with her students, he had to admit that Ms. Walsh's enthusiasm made learning fun. She was generous with attention, encouragement and praise. Her love for kids was so genuine, they all responded to her.

He also had to admit he respected Ms. Walsh for coming all the way out here to apologize to him. He even thought her bringing the cookies and the learning targets had been a nice touch. If she had left it at that, things would have been fine.

But she hadn't done that. No, she'd come inside, made herself at home, criticized him for sending his daughter to bed, and then had the nerve to call Kitty an overly polite, sad little ghost.

Determined to put Ms. Walsh out of his mind, he piled up the learning targets and the Mother's Day gift, thumped them down on a bookcase and went back to his desk. He picked up the file he'd been working on, read the first page, then realized he hadn't digested a single word, slammed it shut and strode back to the family room, muttering choice expletives to himself.

It only took a minute to find the old box of family videotapes. He shoved the first tape into the VCR, braced himself as best he could and pushed the play button.

"Over here, sweetheart. Look at Mommy."

Gina's voice sounded so real on the videotape, Jack almost expected to turn his head and see her sitting beside him. When he hadn't been certain he could go on without her for one more second, much less one more day, he'd watched these videos and pretended she was sitting beside him. He'd talked to her about anything and everything, until he finally realized that he'd rather live in his pretend world with Gina than in the real world with their daughter. Their daughter who needed him.

"Okay, Kitty, sing your song for Daddy," Gina said.

A three-year-old Kitty posed for the camera. When Gina again coaxed her to sing her song, the little imp rolled her eyes like an exasperated teenager, then sang—well, she shouted more than she sang, but what could anyone reasonably expect from a three-year-old?

"I'm a wittwe teapot, shote and stout."

Jack smiled and shook his head at the trouble Kitty had once had pronouncing her *L*'s and her *R*'s.

She jammed one hand on her hip. "Hewe is my handwe." She flopped her other hand out to the side. "And hewe is my spout. When I get all steamed up, then I shout." Kitty bent at the waist, leaning toward her "spout." "Tip me ovew and pouw me out."

"Wonderful," Gina said, zooming in for a close-up of Kitty's face. "Say hi to Daddy."

"Hi, Daddy! I wove you!" Kitty shouted, mugging for the camera again.

Jack watched the rest of that tape and the next one and the next, but long before the last one ended, he knew he had to face some hard truths he hadn't wanted to see because they meant he was failing Kitty.

Dammit, Ms. Walsh was right. He hadn't wanted her to be right about anything, because he couldn't bear the thought of watching Kitty suffer in therapy the way she had before. That was why he'd found Ms. Walsh so irritating, why he didn't want Kitty to like her so much, why he'd fought accepting her suggestions the way he should have done.

He'd been doing his best with Kitty, but his best wasn't good enough. Not even close.

She didn't look or act like the same child anymore, and the change had nothing to do with the age difference. The adorable, funny, happy child in the videotapes was the real Kitty, not the pale, skinny, tired little girl he'd come home to tonight. His Kitty was the one who shouted, "I wove you, Daddy," and held out her little arms for a huge hug.

Jack leaned forward and put his face in his hands. Dear God, he wanted her back. He wanted her to be noisy and laugh and run around like a demented creature. He wanted her to wear him out with her demands of "Do it again, Daddy," the way she had that day at the lake when he'd kept tossing her into the water until she was breathless and his arms had ached.

How on earth had he let things come to this?

"Aw, dammit, Gina," he swore, swiping at his cheeks with the back of his hand. "I'm doing it all wrong, and I don't know how to make it right."

He turned off the TV and VCR, then sat there in the quiet of the family room with his burning eyes shut and his head pounding with questions he couldn't answer. What was he supposed to do now?

Gina had always done what was right for Kitty. So what would she do for their daughter in this situation? "Come on, Gina, tell me what to do," he whispered, burying his face in his hands and trying to form a mental picture of his wife.

Unfortunately, the image that appeared in his mind was all wrong. Instead of Gina's short black hair and loving dark eyes, Ms. Walsh's blond ponytail and ac-

cusing green eyes appeared before him. Her steady
gaze held pity for him, but if the image could speak,
he suspected it would call him an idiot or worse.

He knew what he had to do, but his gut knotted
and an automatic protest sprang to his lips. Ask Ms.
Walsh for help? No way. Even the idea made him
shudder, but he had no other choice.

His number-one priority was taking care of Kitty.
No matter how much he hated doing it, it wouldn't
kill him to swallow his pride. He'd call Ms. Walsh
first thing on Monday morning.

*If you wait, certainly you'll find a way to justify
not calling her.*

Muttering "All right, all right," Jack looked up
Ms. Walsh's phone number and dialed it. The phone
rang three times, and only then did he think to look
at the clock. Damn. It was after midnight. Just as he
was about to hang up, she answered.

"Hello?"

He felt like a jerk, but since he had her on the line,
he might as well get this done. "Ms. Walsh, this is
Jack Granger."

"What time is it?" Her voice was soft and slurry
with sleep, and it had an unnerving, surprisingly sexy
rasp to it.

"I didn't realize it was so late," he said quickly.
"I'll call back in the morning."

"Don't do that," she said with a prodigious yawn.
"I'm awake now. Just give me a second."

He heard a rustling sound and found himself wondering what she wore to bed. Cotton? Silk? Nothing?
Oh, jeez. Before he could ask himself why he was
even thinking about Ms. Walsh in that context, she
came back on the line.

"All right. What do you want, Mr. Granger?"

Thank God she didn't know how loaded that question sounded at the moment. "You were right."

"Excuse me?"

"You heard me," he grumbled, scowling at the squeak of surprise in her voice. "You were right about Kitty. Meet me at the school tomorrow. One o'clock."

Abby blinked. Unable to believe what he'd just said and the dictatorial tone in which he'd said it, she held the receiver away from her ear and silently counted to ten before speaking again—slowly and distinctly. "Tomorrow is Saturday."

"So?" he snapped. "Don't you teachers ever work on weekends?"

"No. We don't." She shifted into the same bright tone she used with first graders. "But you know, if I didn't have plans for tomorrow and you had phrased that as a request instead of an order, I might have been willing to think about making an exception for you."

There was no way he could misunderstand that message. She grinned at the stunned silence on the other end of the line. Oh, she'd give a month's salary to see his face right now. She heard him take a deep breath.

"Ms. Walsh, please—" he said.

He sounded as if his teeth might be gritted.

"—I would sincerely appreciate it if you could find it in your heart to change your plans and meet me in your classroom tomorrow."

"That's much better," she said.

"Then you'll meet with me?"

Hoo-boy, he really sounded steamed. "I'm sorry, but I really can't."

"Why not?"

"I'm signed up for a fun run at Manito Park, and then—"

"Fun run?"

He had a bad habit of interrupting her. "Yes. And I don't intend to miss it."

"What about after the fun run?"

"I'm baby-sitting for the rest of the weekend—not that it's any of your business." It was the price she'd had to pay for Erin's expert opinion about Kitty. "I'm free after school on Monday."

After another long silence, he replied in such a grudging tone that she had to bite her lower lip to stop herself from laughing out loud.

"All right. I'll meet you at the school on Monday afternoon. Say, four o'clock?"

"Fine. Try to be on time. Good night, Mr. Granger."

Without waiting for his reply, she hung up and flopped back on her bed, giggling. Oh, dear, this had to be a difficult time for him but he most definitely did not "play well with others." He really needed to learn that he couldn't run roughshod over other people, including his daughter and his daughter's teacher.

But thank God, he'd finally agreed to get Kitty the help she needed. Now she could let Erin take over, gracefully bow out of the Grangers' lives at the end of the school year and get on with earning her doctorate.

Jack spent the night fitfully rolling around in his bed, rehashing his conversations with Ms. Walsh and worrying about Kitty. By sunrise he gave up all hope of sleeping and dragged himself down to the kitchen. After putting on the coffee, he walked out to the road for the paper, scanning the front page on his way back to the house.

In the lower-right corner he spotted a teaser for a five-mile run to promote women's health programs. He'd bet his next conviction that Ms. Walsh would be there. And so would he. Now that he knew Kitty needed help, he wanted to get on with the process. The sooner the better.

After leaving Kitty with his brother Dan, Jack arrived at Manito Park and made his way to the duck pond, the most logical place to put the finish line. Sure enough, there it was, complete with a big digital clock and a race official calling out individual runner's times as they ran past him.

The jovial atmosphere took him back to his high school and college days when he'd been on the cross-country team. He felt a moment's envy of the participants who were in good enough shape to run an eight-minute mile. It had been a long time since he'd found the time and energy to go for a run. Too long.

Hands in the front pockets of his khakis, he prepared to wait however long it took for Ms. Walsh to straggle in after running five miles. If she actually could run that far.

"Look, there she is," shouted a little boy standing in front of Jack. "Way to go, Ms. Walsh!"

"Thirty-nine minutes and thirty-six seconds," the official called.

Startled, Jack looked at the woman charging toward him and found himself doing a double-take. Her hair was plastered to her head with perspiration and pulled back in the usual ponytail, which was now puffed out in a mass of springy curls. Her face was red and glowing. She wore a white mesh singlet over a black sports bra, a red sweatband across her forehead, purple running shorts that showed off the sexiest pair of legs he'd ever seen and a worn pair of running shoes that proclaimed her to be a dedicated runner.

Man, did she ever look trim and fit. Still, teachers were like nuns and mothers. They weren't supposed to have sexy legs like that, or slim, toned arms. Ms. Walsh ran past him, and he nearly swallowed his tongue. Teachers, mothers and nuns weren't supposed to have tight, round little bottoms that made a man's hands itch, either. He felt like a pervert for even thinking such thoughts about his daughter's teacher, but he'd have to be dead not to react to seeing her showing that much skin. And it sure didn't stop him from liking what he saw.

Ms. Walsh looked so…healthy. So full of life. So damn sexy, he couldn't believe his eyes. Who would've guessed that under her long, flowing skirts and soft, colorful blouses was a body like that? Oh, boy, he had to stop staring at her, stop trying to envision what she might look like completely naked. She already disliked him intensely. If she ever realized he thought she was…hot—oh, he didn't want to go there.

Slowing to a trot, she grabbed a paper cup of water from a volunteer, downed it in one gulp, then took another. She tossed the cups in a trash barrel and ran slowly toward the parking area. Jack called her name and waved one arm.

She glanced around, jogging in place until she spotted him. Ignoring her immediate frown, he hustled to join her. "Nice race," he said when he reached her.

"What are you doing here, Mr. Granger?" she asked, still jogging in place.

"I want to talk to you about Kitty."

"We have an appointment on Monday. Right now, I need to cool down."

With that, she took off, maintaining a steady pace. Cursing under his breath, he went after her. He'd already wasted too much of his time this morning to let her get away from him now. His legs were so much longer than hers, he kept up with her by walking fast.

"Come on," he said. "You've been after me to get Kitty into counseling for a long time. I'm finally ready to do it, and you're not willing to help?"

"Not today," she said. "If you want to help Kitty this weekend, take her out somewhere and have some fun. I'll see you Monday afternoon."

Veering off to the right, she gave him a jaunty wave and ran back toward the duck pond. Jack stood there watching her, anger and confusion warring inside him. And there was something else he couldn't deny—a dose of lust. It was a hell of a time for his damn libido to wake up.

"I am *not* attracted to that woman," he muttered to himself all the way back across town. When he arrived at his brother's duplex, he found Dan, who was three years his junior, out in the garage working on his pickup. Dan wore jeans, hiking boots and a Spokane Police Department T-shirt.

He looked up when Jack entered the garage, showing a smudge of grease on his forehead. "That didn't take long."

Jack shrugged. "Where's Kitty?"

Dan tilted his head toward his neighbor's half of the building. "Marla took the kids to a movie and invited Kitty to go along. They'll be back soon. Did you find Kitty's teacher?"

"Yeah," Jack grumbled, walking around to the front of the truck. "What're you doing?"

"Changing spark plugs." Dan shoved a droplight into Jack's hands and ducked in under the hood. "A little more to the right— Yeah, that's it. So, what happened at the race?"

"That woman wouldn't even talk to me." Jack gave his brother an edited description of his recent encounter with Ms. Walsh. Instead of garnering him the sympathy he expected, the story made his dumb brother burst out laughing.

"Good for her," Dan said. "It's about time."

"About time for what?" Jack demanded.

"For somebody to treat you like you're normal."

"What the hell are you talking about?"

Dan ducked back under the hood. "Everybody's been walking on eggshells around you since Gina died."

"No way," Jack protested.

Dan snorted. "Oh, big time, bro. Everybody felt terrible for you and Kitty. When you were impatient and irritable, we made allowances for you, but it's past time somebody made you mind your manners." He straightened away from the pickup and met Jack's gaze head-on. "That's all Ms. Walsh did, you know."

Jack stared at his brother in slack-jawed disbelief. "You're full of it, Danny. I have excellent manners."

"Not anymore," Dan told him. "You act like

you're the only one with a busy schedule and your time is more valuable than anyone else's.''

"Well, maybe it is," Jack said. "I know you don't always think so, but my job happens to be damn important."

"Yeah, it's important." Dan grabbed another spark plug and leaned over the engine again. "But it's still just a job."

"So, it really doesn't matter that much if I let a few killers and sex offenders slip through the system. Who cares if they're back out on the streets?"

"See? There you go. That's exactly what I mean. You act like it's this big mission and only Jack Granger can—"

"Give me a break."

Dan raised up abruptly, banging his head on the underside of the hood. Cursing, he rubbed the sore spot. "You've had enough breaks. If you don't watch yourself, your ego is going to get completely out of control."

"Cut it out. I'm not like that."

Dan pointed his socket wrench at Jack. "If you believe that, you'd better stop and take a long look at yourself, bro."

"So what are you saying?" Jack tossed his free hand up beside his head. "I shouldn't do my job?"

"Hell, no. You just have to remember you're not the only prosecutor in this county, and you can't be responsible for every conviction. Face it, no matter how many killers you put away, you'll never be able to get the one you really want."

Jack stiffened at the veiled reference to their father. "That's enough."

"Says who? I admire the hell out of that teacher

for not putting up with your bull. You're real good at making people back off from touchy subjects, but you need to hear the truth about these things, even if you don't want to. *Especially* if you don't want to."

"And where did you get your Psych degree? The Police Academy?"

Dan grabbed the last spark plug. "I don't need a Psych degree to figure out any of us. Mark and I are cops because of Dad, and you're a prosecutor because of Dad's killer. There's nothing wrong with that."

"What's your point?"

"My point is, ever since Gina died you've buried yourself in your job. It's not good for you and it's not good for Kitty. And your manners stink."

"What did I ever do to you?" Jack asked. "Give me an example."

"That's easy. When you called this morning, you didn't ask me to take care of Kitty for you—you *told* me to. I didn't have anything more interesting going on this morning, so I didn't mind helping you out this time."

"But you have at other times?"

"Only because you ordered me around like I was ten. I'll bet you did the same thing to Kitty's teacher."

Squirming inwardly, Jack set the light on the workbench. "Not intentionally."

"I know that," Dan said, "but I doubt that teacher does."

Jack looked back over his shoulder at Dan. "What do you suggest I do about it?"

"Well, there's this thing Mom used to talk about—" Dan's eyes glinted with humor. "I think it's called an apology."

"Yeah, yeah," Jack grumbled. Apologies had never come easily for him, but Ms. Walsh had been a big enough person to give him one when she'd crossed the line. He leaned back against Dan's workbench, folded his arms over his chest and crossed one foot over the other, watching Dan check the power steering fluid and then wipe his greasy hands on a shop rag.

"Does Mark feel the same way about me?" Jack asked, referring to the youngest Granger brother.

"Ask him," Dan said.

"That means yes." Jack uttered a grim laugh and shook his head. "It's hard to argue with a unanimous verdict."

"Look, maybe I came down on you too hard," Dan said. "I mean, you're not a total jerk."

"Knowing I'm only a semi-jerk makes me feel much better."

Grinning, Dan punched his arm. "C'mon, you know what I mean. It's just that you're going to need the teacher's help. For Kitty's sake, you can't afford to alienate her."

"I hear you," Jack said. "I'll go see Ms. Walsh on Monday and make nice, and we'll get Kitty back on track."

Dan led the way into his kitchen and poured himself a mug of coffee. "It sounds like Kitty needs more than that. Why don't you take a leave of absence?"

"Are you nuts?" Jack demanded. "How can you even think about saying that?"

"Maybe because your kid needs you?"

"Yeah, I got that part from Ms. Walsh, believe me."

"So, learn to delegate. No time like the present."

Jack helped himself to the coffee. "It's not that easy. I have ongoing cases."

"You took time off when Gina died, and the world survived."

"I'll think about it," Jack said, wondering why everybody else in the world knew what he should be doing better than he did.

Chapter Four

Mr. Granger phoned Abby at noon on Monday and asked if she would mind changing their meeting place to a coffee shop not far from the school. A frequent customer of the establishment, she readily agreed. When the dismissal bell rang, she stuffed a file into her satchel and made a quick stop in the teachers' lounge to freshen her makeup and comb her hair. Then she was out the door and on her way.

To her great surprise, he was already there when she arrived. He stood up and waved to attract her attention. He wore his usual lawyer uniform of a navy, pin-striped suit with a white shirt and a nondescript tie. She could have sworn the once-over he gave her held more than a touch of masculine interest.

Telling herself that that had to be the product of her overactive imagination didn't stop her pulse from stuttering. Or her vain self from being glad that, due to a curriculum meeting at the district office that morning, she'd worn a red, short-sleeved suit with a slim, knee-length skirt instead of one of her long jumpers or slacks outfits. She had no business feeling or thinking anything of that nature as it pertained to him, of course, but her vain self didn't care.

She waved back, calling, "I'll be with you in a minute." After ordering a double-shot, skinny mocha, she discovered he'd already arranged to pay for whatever she wanted. She carried the steaming cup to his booth and slid onto the seat opposite his. "Thanks for the coffee."

"You're welcome. Consider it a peace offering for disturbing you over the weekend. Like those cookies you brought to my house."

Clapping one hand over her heart as if she expected it to fail at any moment, Abby faked a choking cough. "Mr. Granger, is it possible you're actually—" she paused for dramatic effect and lowered her voice to a whisper "—apologizing to me?"

A reluctant-looking grin tugged at the corners of his mouth. "I suppose you could call it that."

She managed to suppress an urge to do a double-take at that, but decided she'd already poked at him enough for the moment. Lacing her fingers around her cup, she said, "I accept."

"Good." He leaned forward, his expression and his voice so earnest that she couldn't doubt his sincerity. "I'm willing to try counseling again for Kitty. Give me the list of people you recommend, and I'll set up an appointment for her."

Who *was* this guy? she wondered, feeling down-right giddy from the way his blue eyes, minus their usual frost, studied her face without the slightest hint of impatience or hostility.

"You did say you'd help me," he prompted.

"Yes, of course," she said, hoping she hadn't been staring at him like an idiot, but fearing that she had. "And I will. Did the learning targets change your mind?"

He leaned back against the bench, thoughtfully shaking his head. "No. I studied them, of course, but that wasn't it."

"May I ask what did?"

"Does it matter?"

"Not really. It's just that you seem so different and, well…agreeable. I find myself wanting to say, 'Who are you? And what have you done with the real Mr. Granger?'"

"Ha ha. Very funny," he said with a frown and just enough of his old impatience to convince her that the infamous body-snatchers hadn't paid him a visit. "Yes, I changed my mind. Enjoy it now because it doesn't happen often."

Abby chuckled. "It didn't hurt, did it?"

That reluctant grin tugged at his mouth again, but it didn't reach his eyes. "Don't push your luck, lady."

She took a sip from her coffee. "Seriously, I was wondering if perhaps something happened between you and Kitty on Friday after I left. And, I'll probably have to change another parent's mind someday. It'd be nice to know what worked."

"You mean there are other parents who don't give in to your steamroller tactics? I'm amazed."

He actually smiled at her this time. As smiles went, it was pitifully restrained, but the corners of his mouth definitely curved up and the outer corners of his eyes crinkled. Her pulse actually lurched. Oh, she'd been so right about what a difference a smile would make in his appearance. Not that she really noticed. For heaven's sake, his looks didn't matter. She was a professional and he was a student's *father*.

"It was what you said about seeing the little girl Kitty used to be," he said, his voice filled with regret. "I remembered the home videos my wife had made. I watched them after you left and realized I'd forgotten a lot about what Kitty was like back then."

Unable to remain emotionally neutral after an admission like that, Abby said softly, "That must have been painful for you. I'm sorry."

He shrugged. "Don't be. I'm grateful you cared enough about Kitty to pursue the matter. I suppose a thank-you is in order."

Though he'd been acting more cordial than usual this afternoon and he'd said it somewhat grudgingly, that thank-you simply was too much for her to swallow. Especially coming from him. "Are you all right, Mr. Granger?"

Surging to his feet, he shoved his hands in his trouser pockets and looked down at her, his body radiating tension. "Look, we haven't started out very well."

"You might say that," Abby drawled, not surprised to hear more impatience in his voice.

"Part of that's probably my fault."

Did he seriously expect her to pass up an opening like that one? "Probably?"

He shot her a fierce scowl that nearly made her laugh out loud. Then, as if remembering he had some purpose in mind, here, he shut his eyes for a moment, inhaled deeply and released the breath before looking at her again. "Do you think we could start over on a more friendly basis?"

"I certainly started out that way, Mr. Granger."

"That's a good example of what I'm trying to get at." He braced his palms on the top of the booth seat and leaned down, bringing his eyes almost to the same level as hers. "Last week you said we were supposed to be on the same side, but if that's true, calling each other Mr. Granger and Ms. Walsh seems awfully formal."

"As I recall, that was *your* choice. I simply followed your example."

"You're right. But do you think you could call me Jack from now on? It's a small step, but we have to start somewhere if we want to change things."

The smile he leveled at her was warm enough to melt an igloo. In the Arctic. In January.

Abby's insides fluttered, and every feminine instinct she possessed went on full alert. Who would have dreamed that underneath that grumpy exterior lurked such potential for charm? She wasn't buying it, of course.

After nearly an entire school year of defensiveness, suspicion and occasional hostility from him, she had a hard time believing he honestly wanted to cooperate, let alone be friends.

"I don't know why you want to do this," she said slowly, "but for Kitty, I'll call you Pinocchio if that'll make you happy. And you can call me Abby."

Straightening to his full height, he studied her, the intensity of his gaze making her nervous. "Thanks...Abby."

Her first name sounded odd coming from his lips,

but still, she liked it. Hoping it didn't show, she pointed toward the other bench seat. "Now then, if you'll sit back down, let's discuss what we're going to do for Kitty."

He slid back into his side of the booth. "Have you noticed you're always telling me to sit down?"

"That's because I don't like people towering over me."

When he again was seated across from her, she took a deep breath to clear her head, then began. "We have an excellent social worker on staff here at Mountain View. She's done extensive work with grieving children. The service is free, and Kitty could see her during the school day, so it would be convenient for you."

"No," he said, immediately shaking his head. "I don't want to do that."

"Are you going to go right back to disagreeing with everything I suggest?" Abby asked.

"No. I just don't want that sort of information to go into her school records and follow her for the next eleven years."

"I understand your concern," Abby said. "I also agree with it. Even some educated people can be surprisingly ignorant about counseling."

Leaning down to hide a smile at his flaring nostrils, she pulled the yellow file folder out of her satchel and removed the top sheet of paper from inside. She handed it across the table. "This is a list of the local therapists I normally recommend for my students."

"How often do you have to do that?" he asked.

"More often than you might think," she replied. "There are usually at least one or two children in my class who need some help."

Frowning, he studied the names. "I've never heard of any of these people. If Kitty was your daughter, who would you choose?"

"Erin Johnson," Abby said without the slightest hesitation. "I've known her for a long time. She does a lot of play therapy with children, and she's gotten some amazing results with my students."

"How long does it take?"

"That varies from child to child. It depends on how often they meet, how severe the problem is and how accessible the child's emotions are."

"What do you mean by 'accessible'?"

Abby bit back a sigh of relief. This was more like it. A simple exchange of information between teacher and parent, with no hidden agendas. Until this moment, she hadn't known if she was capable of having such a normal conversation with him.

"It's just how aware they are of their feelings and how well they can articulate them," she said. "I suspect Kitty's emotions may be fairly close to the surface."

Jack ran his fingers through his hair in obvious frustration. "Is that a good thing or a bad thing?"

"Erin will be able to tell us. I believe Kitty's trying to give me her Mother's Day gift was a cry for help." He seemed so worried by that, she gave him what she hoped was a reassuring smile. "That's a good thing."

"I hope you're right."

She leaned forward, resting her forearms on the table and clasping her hands together while she studied his face. "You're still not happy about doing this, are you."

"I'm not happy about the *need* for doing this." He

grimaced. "I should have seen what was happening to her."

"Not necessarily. When a child loses a parent, it's hard to know what's really 'normal' behavior. In Kitty's case, being sad and upset for a long time was a perfectly reasonable response."

"She was that, all right."

"Some of the other changes in her behavior probably happened very gradually, over a period of months. And you had your own grief to deal with. Even if you missed something, it won't do her any good if you beat yourself up with guilt now."

He gazed at her for a moment, opened his mouth as if he would speak, hesitated, then closed it again.

"What were you going to say?" she asked.

"You wouldn't believe me if I told you," he grumbled, abruptly glancing away.

"I might. Why don't you try it and see?"

He gave her an abashed, nearly boyish grin that charmed her far more than that killer smile he'd used on her earlier. "What do you say we get out of here and take a walk around that park across the street?"

It was the last thing she'd expected, but she was eager to get out into the fresh air. "Sure. Why not?"

They left the coffee shop quickly, stopped at their cars to store their things and met up again on the sidewalk. Jack put his hand on the small of her back as they hurried across Waikiki Road. He lowered his hand to his side again when they entered Holmberg Park, and she felt an irrational twinge of regret. Oh, dear, she really had to get her hormones under control.

Breathing deeply, Abby ambled along beside him, giving him a lap around the playground equipment to collect his thoughts. For the first time, the silence between them felt companionable rather than tense. He seemed as big as ever, but no longer intimidating. She appreciated the way he shortened his stride to match hers. Glancing up at him, she caught him studying her with an expression she could only call perplexed.

"What?" she asked. "Whatever it is, I can handle it."

A deep, rusty-sounding chuckle rumbled out of him, warming her like the late-afternoon sunshine. "I think you can probably handle almost anything. I'm just not sure how to say this."

"That must be an odd experience for a prosecutor."

"It is." He chuckled again and shook his head in apparent bemusement. "Believe me, it is."

"I prefer blunt," Abby said. "It saves time."

"All right. I really do want to apologize."

"For what?"

"Isn't that obvious?"

"Not to me," she said. "We've had so many missed communications this past year, I'd prefer to have everything spelled out."

He jerked at the knot in his tie and unbuttoned the top button of his white shirt, then unbuttoned his sleeves and rolled them halfway to his elbows. "For being rude last Friday. For bothering you on the weekend. For everything."

"All right," she said.

"I never meant to be argumentative or uncooperative," he went on. "It's just that when it comes to Kitty, I'm out of my depth. Most of the time I don't know what I'm doing, and I tend to act defensive. Pathetic, isn't it?"

She stopped walking, and waited until he stopped and looked back at her. "Don't you know most parents feel that way? Especially with a first child?"

"My wife always knew what she was doing with Kitty." He stuck his hands into his front trouser pockets and started walking again. Guessing it was easier for him to talk when he was moving, she hurried to catch up.

"She was such a great mother, I just let her handle everything," he continued. "When she died, well, I'm sure you've noticed I'm not going to win any Father of the Year awards."

"I don't make judgments like that about other people."

"Come on, be honest. If it wasn't for my bumbling, Kitty wouldn't be having all these problems. You know that as well as I do."

"No." She shook her head adamantly. "Depression can happen to anyone. I've had students with two attentive, loving parents, no traumas anyone knew of, and yet they've still suffered from depression. Given what you and Kitty have been through, it's hardly surprising that she'd have some adjustment problems, no matter what you did or didn't do."

He shot her a doubtful glance. "You're not just saying that to make me feel better?"

"I don't like you enough to do that." She grinned at the startled look on his face and joined him when he chuckled again. "I've thought you were abrasive, hardheaded and extremely frustrating at times, but I've never doubted that you loved Kitty. For me, that's the main requirement for a good father."

He was silent for a moment. "Thanks. You're a very generous woman."

"Don't mention it, Jack." It was the first time she'd said his name. She suspected he was every bit as aware of it as she was, but he didn't so much as blink in reaction.

"All right, Abby. I'll call Dr. Johnson in the morning."

He paused near the chain-link fence surrounding the empty swimming pool. "Now, about Kitty's schoolwork."

"What about it?"

"After reading all those learning targets, I don't see how she can catch up with her class by the end of the year."

"I doubt that she will," Abby admitted. "It'll help if you continue to work with her during the summer, of course."

"But what about promoting her to the second grade?"

Abby considered his question. "I think the therapy's more important. Once she starts to make progress there, the schoolwork will probably take care of itself. She's awfully bright."

"Don't you think being left behind her class will hurt her self-esteem? Especially if the other kids tease her next year?"

"That's a possibility."

"Well, isn't there *something* else we can do to help her catch up?"

"If her therapy goes well, you could hire a private tutor to work with her over the summer. We could set up a conditional promotion, and if she's ready for second grade in the fall, she can move on with her class. I can recommend some good tutors for you, too."

He thought about it for a moment, then abruptly shook his head. "I don't think that's a good idea."

"Why not?" Abby did her best to hide her exasperation. Honestly, even when he was being nice and cooperative, he was difficult. "You just said you don't see how she can catch up and you don't want her to be left behind."

"I didn't mean she shouldn't have a tutor." Jack stuck his hands in his front trouser pockets and started walking again. "She's already going to be coping with one new adult in her life with the therapist. I don't think she should have to deal with another one at the same time."

"Unless you have someone else in mind, or you can take a lot of time off work this summer, I don't see any alternative."

He grinned. "Why don't *you* be her tutor?"

"Oh, I, uh, well..." she sputtered. "I just couldn't."

"You know how, don't you?"

"Of course. I've even done it before, but—"

"Then, you could do it again." His voice took on an infectious enthusiasm. "In fact, you're the most logical person to do it. You know exactly what she needs to learn, and Kitty would love working with you."

She looked up into his eyes and found herself on the receiving end of another one of his knee-weakening, heart-tripping smiles. Taking a step back, she bumped into a picnic table. He grasped her elbow to steady her.

The contact between his fingers and her bare arm made her acutely aware of him—his size, his strength, his sheer masculinity. It was ridiculous, of course.

Just because he smiled at her and prevented her from falling down didn't mean he thought of her as anything more than his daughter's teacher.

She didn't want him to, either. She wasn't even in the market for a new man in her life and doubted she ever would be. She liked him better surly; this nicer man confused her and disrupted her equilibrium.

Abruptly turning away, she started walking across the grass back toward the playground equipment. Realizing he wasn't following her, she turned back around to face him, and caught him in the act of quickly raising his gaze. Good heavens, had he been looking at her bottom or her legs? A flush high on his cheekbones confirmed her suspicion.

Her stomach flip-flopped at the idea. Oh, she must have imagined it. Even if she hadn't, she had to think and act like a professional.

"That's flattering," she said, "but I have other things I have to do this summer."

"What other things?"

"I'll be writing my doctoral dissertation for one."

"That sounds impressive. What's your topic?" He put his hands on his hips and moved his feet wider apart.

This was *not* a good time for her to notice his broad shoulders or his flat belly. For pity's sake, she was twenty-eight, not fifteen. "Children's learning styles based on their personality types."

"Is that all you have left to do for your doctorate?"

"Yes," she said with a nod, forcing herself to look away from him.

A young couple ambled by on the sidewalk. They were holding hands, and the man was carrying a baby in a backpack. The image wrenched her heart. She started walking again, heading for the sidewalk this time.

"Well, there you have it," he said, joining her. "You can't write all day and all evening. Surely you could spare an hour a day for Kitty."

Abby shook her head. "No, really. I'm going to be busy, and I don't think it's a good idea to allow Kitty to become too attached to me."

They reached the sidewalk and stopped to wait for a break in the traffic.

"How about a compromise?" he asked.

"What do you have in mind?"

"If you could just get Kitty used to being tutored, then we could gradually work in someone else. By the end of July, she'll be comfortable with Dr. Johnson, and she'll be more able to accept a replacement for you."

Though she could see the wisdom of his plan, Abby still hesitated. She already adored Kitty. Today she'd met a Jack Granger she actually could talk to and, yes, even like. Not to mention all the flickers of attraction she'd been feeling toward him, ridiculous or not.

She couldn't deny that the Grangers needed help and she wanted to give it to them. But while her heart belonged to any child in need, this situation held all the ingredients for an emotional disaster.

For as long as she could remember, Abby had dreamed of having a family of her own. Unfortunately she, herself had been something of a miracle baby, and she'd inherited her mother's infertility problems. Based on her father's and her ex-husband's reactions, Abby had reached the decision that she'd never again have anything more than a casual relationship with a man.

Jack and Kitty had lost a wife and a mother, and it was oh-so-easy to imagine herself stepping in, filling those roles and loving every moment. She might get away with it for a while. But one day Jack would realize he wanted a second child she couldn't give him.

Focusing on her career was a safer, saner course of action. Getting her bachelor's degree, then her master's and now her doctorate had been a long, hard pull for her. Writing her dissertation would be no easy task, and she'd be getting ready to move at the end of August, as well. Oh, she just wasn't ready to make this decision.

"Please," Jack said, "you've already done so much for Kitty. Couldn't you do this one last job to make all of these new things she's got to face a little easier for her?"

"You must've been a salesman in another life." He'd made a convincing argument, but she still wasn't ready to commit herself to anything. "I'll think about it."

He hustled her across the street and escorted her to her Bronco. "Will you really think about it?"

"Yes. If you don't keep hammering at me, I'll seriously think about it."

"Is that your final answer?"

"It's the best offer you're going to get from me today."

"All right, Abby." He said her name with a warm smile and an inflection in his voice that suggested he liked saying it. "Thanks for your time and your advice."

He crossed the parking lot to his car, whistling all the way. Struggling not to overreact to that smile, Abby climbed into her sport-utility vehicle, started the engine and drove away. Jack obviously thought he already had her convinced.

If she were honest, she'd have to admit he could be right. Could she turn away from Kitty at this point? Not likely. Still, she couldn't help thinking that committing herself to that much contact with the Grangers could be a big mistake. Erin had been concerned about her getting too involved with them. Maybe she should listen to her friend this time.

Then again, maybe not.

Chapter Five

Acting on impulse, Jack stopped at a nursery and bought bedding plants on his way home from meeting with Abby. By the time he finished, flats of petunias, pansies, snapdragons, marigolds and impatiens in every shade imaginable filled the trunk and the back seat of his sedan. Buyer's remorse set in as soon as he pulled out of the parking lot.

He didn't have time for gardening. He'd always enjoyed the flowers Gina had planted every spring, but they'd been her doing, not his. He shouldn't have bought all this stuff, but it had been a long, nasty winter and a cold, rainy spring. Now the sunshine finally had returned. The grass had turned green again. Tulips and daffodils were blooming, their bright colors providing a welcome break from the dreary days that had lasted so long.

He and Kitty needed to tap into some of that color

and energy nature was producing. They needed to stop looking back at all they'd lost and start looking forward to what they could build for themselves in the future. What better place to start doing that than in their flower beds? Maybe they should even plant a vegetable garden out back.

Whatever they decided, he was going to use the plants to spend time with Kitty. The flower beds wouldn't be as perfect as they'd been when Gina had tended them, but he and Kitty would have something fun to do together. They hadn't had nearly enough of that lately.

Millie fussed at him for being late, until she saw the flowers he'd bought. She gasped, folded her hands together and clutched them to her bosom, a delighted smile lending youth and beauty to her lined face. "What a good idea, Jack. Kitty will love them. They're for her, aren't they?"

"She's going to help me with them," he said. "I want to get her away from the TV."

Millie nodded enthusiastically, then reached out to take a flat of pansies from him and set it on the workbench. "That's a fine idea. It'll do her good to spend more time outdoors. My old knees can't take so much planting anymore, but if you'll get those flowers in the ground, I'll teach Kitty how to tend them."

"Thanks. I knew I could count on you, Millie."

"I'm always happy to do whatever I can for you and that precious child, dear. Now let me help unload the car, then I'm off to have dinner with my sister."

"Dinner" was Millie's euphemism for her weekly adventure with her sister, playing the slot machines at a Native American casino in Chewelah. She won a surprising amount of money on these excursions and she seemed to have a sixth sense telling her when it was time to quit.

"Hitting the slots again, huh?" Jack said with a grin.

"Just you wait. One of these days I'll hit a big jackpot and retire."

"But what would we do without you?"

She flushed with pleasure. "You'd survive, dear. And maybe you'd start looking for a lady friend. That child still needs a mother, you know."

Unwilling to touch that remark, Jack just smiled and carried the last flat of flowers to the workbench. He waited for Millie to collect her purse, walked her to her car and opened the door for her. "Thanks for the help." They both knew he wasn't talking about the plants. "Have fun tonight, and good luck."

Millie patted the hand he'd rested on her open window. "You too, dear. You too."

He walked back to the house, then went to look for Kitty. Once again he found her curled up in front of the TV. Gina would be appalled to know Kitty was well on her way to becoming a couch potato. Well, he was about to fix that.

"Hi, Kitten," he said.

"Hi, Daddy," she murmured without looking at him.

He walked in front of her and turned off the TV. She frowned at him, but didn't protest. Jeez, she was getting so apathetic, she hardly reacted to anything anymore. That had to stop—the sooner the better.

Turning back to the sofa, he scooped her into his arms, draped her over his shoulder and carried her out of the room. She screeched in surprise, then let out a soft giggle that warmed his heart. He hadn't heard her do that since Abby had eaten cookies with her.

"What are you *doing,* Daddy?" she asked, clutching at the back of his shirt.

"I've got a surprise for my kitten."

"What kinda surprise?"

"If I told you, it wouldn't be a surprise."

"Well, where are you taking me?"

"Upstairs to change out of your school clothes."

"How come?"

"Because we're going to get dirty. Really dirty."

He set her on her feet outside her bedroom. "I have to change, too. Put on something old and meet me in the kitchen. Last one downstairs is a rotten egg."

She gave him a semi-smile, went into her room and shut the door. He hurriedly changed into jeans, a T-shirt and a pair of his old running shoes, waiting until he heard Kitty come out of her room and tromp down the stairs before leaving his own room.

He'd hoped she would laugh and call him a rotten egg, but she just stood beside the table, watching him with big, sad eyes and waiting quietly for him to join her.

Would she ever feel free to talk to him? Tease him? Laugh at him? Maybe in time. With the help of the therapist and Abby, surely Kitty would open up. Please, God, let her open up and be that little imp on the home videotapes again.

They carried the flowers to the front yard, choosing the ones they would plant in the beds on either side of the front steps. Kitty followed him around without much eagerness, but he did his best to provide enough enthusiasm for both of them. It took three trips to get everything they needed.

He gave her a small trowel to dig in the dirt on the right side of the steps, while he took the shovel, turned over the earth and broke up the dirt clods in the bed to the left of the steps. She worked silently, a frown wrinkling her forehead, an occasional sigh escaping her pursed lips. The shovel's blade clunked against something. He squatted down, ran his fingers through the loosened dirt and came up with a small plastic figure of a woman wearing a yellow dress. Smiling, he held it up to show Kitty.

"Look, Kitten, it's your Mrs. Lady. Remember her?"

Kitty glanced at the little doll, then shrugged and went back to her own digging.

Jack carried the toy across the yard and squatted beside her. "She was part of the family that came with a house and a little red car. You called them Mrs. Lady, Mr. Man, Brother Boy and Sister Girl, and you used to carry them around and play with them all the time. Remember?"

She wrinkled her nose at him and looked back down at the weeds. "Sorta."

"How do you suppose she got in the garden?"

"Dunno."

He saw Kitty's throat contract and heard her swallow, but she kept her gaze focused on the ground. "I'll bet you were out here helping Mommy plant flowers, just like we're doing now. You really liked doing that with her."

Jerking her head up, she looked at him, her eyes wide and rapidly filling with tears.

"Hey, what's wrong, Kitten?" he said, surprised by her reaction.

He reached for her a second too late. She scrambled

to her feet and ran headlong up the steps and into the house. He ran after her, but she made it to her bedroom first and slammed the door in his face. He'd never wanted anything more than he wanted to go in there and comfort her, but he feared that would be an invasion of her privacy. Or that somehow he would make matters worse.

Frozen with indecision, he stood in the hallway, listening to her weep and feeling as if his heart was ripping right down the middle. Finally, unable to stand it another second, he went in. She lay on her stomach in the middle of her bed, her whole body shaking with the force of her sobs.

He knelt beside the bed and hesitantly stroked the back of her head with an unsteady hand. "Shh, Kitty. It's all right. Don't cry, baby."

"Go 'way, Daddy," she wailed into her pillow.

"I can't leave when you're so upset."

"Go *'way!*" She reached out blindly and made a shoving motion, as if she would push him away if she could see what she was doing.

Devastated, Jack got to his feet, his knees creaking like an old man's. "If that's what you want," he said. "I'm sorry if I…well, I'll be downstairs if you need me. I'll come back up and check on you in a little while."

He closed the door on his way out, leaned back against it and took a deep breath. Damn. Kitty hadn't had an outburst like that in a long time. What was it about Mrs. Lady that had set her off? God, he hoped he could get her in to see the therapist soon.

But what could he do for Kitty right now? *Call Abby.* The thought was immediate and impossible to ignore. It probably was inappropriate as hell to ask a teacher for this kind of help, but he couldn't think of anyone better equipped to calm Kitty down.

Abby answered her phone on the first ring. He explained what had happened, hung up, checked on Kitty, then went downstairs to wait.

When Abby arrived fifteen minutes later, he stepped out onto the front porch. Wearing a pair of denim shorts with an old teal Bloomsday T-shirt and a pair of leather sandals, she hurried to the house. Her hair was down around her shoulders, her face scrubbed clean of makeup. She looked about fifteen years old, but no one had ever looked any better to him than she did at that moment. Relief washed over him like a warm summer rain.

"Thanks for coming," he said.

She climbed the steps, her forehead creased with concern. "How is she?"

"Last time I checked on her, she was still sobbing." He led Abby inside and showed her Mrs. Lady. "She started crying when I found this, but I don't know why."

Abby took the little plastic woman from Jack and studied her. It was nothing special, just part of a common toy set sold by every discount store chain for years. Erin's children and thousands of American children owned that tiny plastic family.

"Will you try to find out?" Jack asked.

Nodding, Abby gave him back the toy, then hurried through the living room and up the stairs to Kitty's bedroom.

"Kitty?" Abby called, knocking on the door. "It's Ms. Walsh, honey. I'm going to come in and talk to you. Okay?"

She heard a loud sniffle, then a soft "'Kay."

Abby turned the doorknob and slipped into the room, closing the door behind her. Kitty lay on the bed, curled into a fetal position, her body shaking with the force of her sobs. Heart breaking for the child, Abby crossed the room and sat on the side of the bed.

Without hesitation, she gathered Kitty into her arms and tried to pull the little girl onto her lap. While Kitty was small for her age, she was big enough to make the maneuver difficult for Abby. Somehow she managed it, however, and Kitty buried her face in Abby's shoulder, flung one arm around Abby's neck and clung as if she expected to be pushed away.

"It's all right. It's all right. Go ahead and cry it all out, sweetie." Abby lost track of time, rocking Kitty, patting her, cuddling her and crooning to her, until Abby's arms ached with fatigue and Kitty ran out of tears and sobs.

"Can you tell me what's wrong, Kitty?"

Fervently shaking her head, Kitty kept her face buried in Abby's shoulder.

"Not at all?" Abby asked.

Kitty shook her head again, but didn't speak or look up.

Abby gave her a few minutes to rest before trying again. "I feel really sad to see you so upset, sweetie. Whatever is bothering you, I promise I'll understand. And if I understand, maybe I can do something to help you."

Exhaling a deep, shuddering sigh, Kitty mumbled, "No. You can't help. You can't help."

"I'll bet your daddy could."

"No. Daddy can't. Daddy can't." An hysterical note sharpened Kitty's voice. "No."

"Why not, sweetie? Your daddy's a pretty smart guy, and he sure loves you. He'd do anything for you."

"Daddy can't," Kitty insisted, pulling away from Abby far enough to look at her from puffy, reddened eyes. Then a strangled cry came out of her throat, and her little face crumpled into a mask of anguish. "Mommy. Mommy. I w-want m-my M-Mommyyyy."

She started crying as if she'd completely refilled her supply of tears and sobs. Feeling as though her heart were in her throat, Abby gathered the child close and set about comforting her as best she could. This definitely was a job for Erin, and with Jack's permission, Abby intended to convince her friend that there was no time to waste. Kitty simply couldn't wait two weeks for a regular appointment to open up in Erin's schedule.

An eternity later, the little girl quieted to sniffles and occasional hiccups. Abby wiped her eyes, dug a clean tissue out of her shorts pocket, wiped Kitty's cheeks and told her to blow her nose. Then, Abby helped the exhausted child get into her pajamas and took her into the bathroom to wash her face, comb her hair out and brush her teeth.

Jack was waiting for them when they stepped back into the hallway. He knelt down in front of Kitty, his eyes filled with love and anxious concern as he searched her little face.

"Are you feeling better now, Kitten?" he asked, tucking a lock of hair behind her ear.

She gave him a jerky nod. "Uh-huh."

"I'm glad to hear that. Looks like you're all ready for bed."

Kitty nodded again. "Ms. Walsh is gonna read me some stories."

"That sounds nice. Do you mind if I come in and listen, too?"

Kitty eyed him with a doubtful expression for a moment, then put her arms around his neck and hugged him. "Okay."

They all went into Kitty's room. Kitty handed a stack of storybooks to Abby, climbed onto her bed and sat with her back braced against the wall. Abby sat close beside her, her feet hanging over the edge of the mattress.

Jack took a spot on the floor directly across the room from Abby. He smiled at her as she reached for the first book. She felt warmed by the gratitude in his eyes and the sense that they were sharing an extremely important mission—saving Kitty.

After four stories Kitty's eyes began to droop. In the middle of the fifth one they closed altogether, and she sagged against Abby like a sack of oatmeal. Jack went to the bed and lifted her. Abby gathered up the books and folded the covers back. When Jack lay Kitty on the sheet, Abby pulled the covers over her, tucking them around Kitty's neck and shoulders with loving pats.

Bending down, Jack kissed Kitty's forehead, hovering over her as if he desperately wished he knew some way to make everything in her little world all right. Abby watched him from the doorway, her heart pinching at the tenderness in his eyes as he gazed at his daughter's sweet, innocent face.

He straightened up and came toward her, his expression carefully masked. Oh, dear. She'd been so focused on Kitty, she hadn't noticed what Jack was wearing.

Well-washed jeans hugged his long legs and butt, and a pale blue T-shirt clung to his broad shoulders and chest. The casual clothes looked every bit as good on him in reality as they had in her imagination. Her mouth went dry and her pulse lost its smooth, steady rhythm, bouncing around like the hyperactive frog she'd once kept in her classroom.

Suddenly conscious of how big and quiet his house was, how alone they were now that Kitty was fast asleep, she turned around and headed for the hallway. He caught up with her in three steps and silently accompanied her to the main floor. At the bottom of the stairs, he said, "Let's talk in the family room so we don't wake her up."

She really should go home, but, of course, he'd want to know what Kitty had told her. She nodded, then nearly jumped out of her skin when he put his hand on the small of her back to guide her in the right direction.

"Relax," he said, a smile in his voice. "I'm not planning to jump you."

Mortified, Abby walked ahead of him, his palm print heating her skin through her clothes. "I didn't think you were."

He gestured to the brown, overstuffed sofa facing a built-in entertainment center. She sat at the far end, tucking one foot under her. Sitting at the other end, he rubbed his eyes with his fingertips, then looked straight at her, strain and weariness evident in every line of his face.

"I don't know how to thank you for coming here tonight. She didn't want me anywhere near her, and...honest to God, I didn't know what else to do. Did she tell you what upset her?''

Abby shook her head. "In fact, the more I pushed about that, the more hysterical she got. She didn't start to calm down until I stopped talking and just held her. You definitely should tell Erin Johnson about this.''

"I'll do that.'' He leaned forward and braced his elbows on his thighs, lacing his fingers together between his knees. "Kitty did this a lot and had nightmares every night when she went to therapy before. It kills me when she won't let me comfort her. I don't know if I can stand going through this again.''

"I don't think you have any choice,'' Abby said quietly. "Something's obviously eating her alive. We've got to figure out what it is and take care of it right away. Otherwise, it could haunt her clear into adulthood.''

"I can see that now.'' Sighing, Jack shook his head, then straightened. "But I don't know what I'm going to do if this takes months and months.''

"It might do that. Do you have any family who could help you?''

"Two brothers. They baby-sit sometimes, but they're both bachelors, and both cops with weird schedules. And they're as helpless as I am when Kitty falls apart.''

"What about her grandmothers?''

"They live out-of-state.''

"You've really been on your own.''

"Lots of single parents are.'' He turned to face her. "You're so good with her. I know this is a terrible imposition, but if this happens again could I call you for help?''

"You should discuss that with Erin. I adore Kitty, but I really am leery of letting her get too attached to me. She needs to depend more on you."

He put his head in his hands, looking so dejected that she wanted to cry for him. Then he raised his head and, with the haunted eyes of a man nearing the end of his emotional resources, looked straight at her. His voice suddenly sounded hoarse. "You're the only adult she's ever turned to since Gina died."

Abby's stomach clenched. Lord, she didn't want to know that. Ever since she'd left Jack at the coffee shop, she'd been talking herself out of tutoring Kitty, and doing a fine job of it. But now...well, there was no escape. Kitty really needed her. So did Jack. She couldn't turn her back on either of them when they were in a crisis.

"Hey, I understand if you don't want to do it for me," he said. "But please, Abby, do it for Kitty."

"It's all right," she said, hearing a hoarse note in her own voice. "I'll do whatever I can for both of you."

His eyes lit with hope. "You'll tutor her?"

"Yes, but I have two conditions."

"Name them."

"I'm only going to tutor her until the end of July. I'll start phasing in my replacement as soon as we can agree on one."

"Okay. What else?"

"You'll come to the school picnic and play day next week and participate in the games with Kitty."

"I accept." He smiled at her then, a smile of such openness and sincerity that it reached down inside her and gave her heart a vigorous wrench. "I was planning to be there, anyway."

Time to leave. Abby rose. "Yeah, that's what they all say, but half of them chicken out the day of the picnic."

"I promise I'll be there."

Abby was acutely aware of him beside her, even though he wasn't touching her as they crossed the entry hall. He rested his hand on the doorknob, his gaze on her face. Then, with no warning whatsoever, he put his hands on her shoulders, turned her to face him and pulled her into a fervent hug, nearly mashing her nose against his upper abdomen.

His T-shirt smelled of soap, and the warmth of his body enveloped her in a wonderful sensation of safety and affection that she hadn't felt in years. Not since before her marriage had gone sour, in fact. Part of her wanted to wrap her arms around him and hug him back, but, of course, that wouldn't be appropriate.

Not at all.

"Thanks, Abby." He touched her lower lip with his thumb in a brief caress before slowly releasing her. "Thanks for everything."

She stepped away, refusing to meet his eyes and hoping she didn't look as discombobulated as she felt. It had only been a hug, after all. How was she supposed to know if it meant anything or not?

Oh, dear. She really should have listened to Erin's warning. But it was too late now. As usual.

"I'll, um…see you next week," she said.

She bolted down the steps, crossed the yard and scrambled into her Bronco. Driving away, she smacked the side of her fist on the steering wheel, muttering, "Good Lord, Abby, what have you gotten yourself into now?"

* * *

Jack stood on the front porch, watching Abby's taillights fade and then disappear when she made the turn onto the road. He probably shouldn't have hugged her like that, but he was so relieved to know he didn't have to handle Kitty's problems by himself, he hadn't been able to stop himself.

It wasn't like him to be so impulsive, but whenever Abby Walsh was around, he wasn't quite himself. She really kept him on his toes. He felt more awake and alive when he was with her, his senses were sharper, everything had more color and texture.

And he didn't feel alone.

How had he ever thought her annoying? After observing her with Kitty tonight, he'd probably believe her if she told him she walked on water. Abby loved Kitty, he was sure of it, and Kitty made no secret of her feelings for Abby.

Suddenly it hit him from out of nowhere. Kitty had lost her mother. Millie thought Kitty needed a new mother, and now he was inclined to agree. The solution was so simple, he couldn't believe he hadn't thought of it before now.

Abby was the answer to Kitty's problems. She was warm and nurturing and knew a lot about children. She'd make a terrific mother for Kitty or any other child. All he had to do was marry her, and his life finally would get back to at least a semblance of normalcy.

Yeah, that would work. Marry Abby. Solve Kitty's problems. Solve his own problems and get a sexy wife in the bargain. Even if she did annoy him at times, there was no problem with physical attraction. Not on his part, anyway.

He didn't think Abby was indifferent to him, either, though he couldn't say whether that was his ego or his instincts talking. It wouldn't hurt to check it out. Subtly, of course. It might even be fun. What a concept.

He'd be so smooth and charming, she'd never know what hit her.

Chapter Six

"Abby, you sandbagger," Erin murmured with a laugh.

Setting the tray of ketchup and mustard bottles she'd been carrying on a picnic table beside the school's barbecue pit, Abby raised her eyebrows at her friend. "What are you talking about?"

"You never told me Grumpface Granger was drop-dead gorgeous." Erin grinned and made a fanning motion with one hand. "Whoowee, the back view must be as good as the front view. Would you look at that row of open mouths behind him?"

Forcing herself to remain relaxed and casual, Abby muttered out the side of her mouth, "Where?"

"Two o'clock. Way over there on the sidewalk by the parking lot. How could you call him Grump-face?"

"He acted like one." Abby spotted Jack and Kitty

walking hand in hand and, in spite of what she'd just said, barely suppressed an appreciative sigh of her own.

Now that she'd made peace with him and liked him better, she'd have to say Jack's looks improved every time she saw him. His crimson-and-gray, Washington State Cougars T-shirt tucked into a tight pair of indigo jeans showcased his tall, rangy build to perfection. The breeze ruffled his dark hair, and the gentle smile he directed at his daughter made him look young, incredibly masculine and impossibly handsome at the same time. She wasn't about to admit any of that to Erin, however.

"Down, girl," Abby teased. "Remember you're married."

"Married, but not dead." Jack and Kitty walked past them on their way to the front door, giving Erin a look at the "back view," and her own jaw dropped open. "Or blind. Oh, thank heaven I can see."

"Right." Abby grinned in sympathy. "Well, close your mouth before your children see you drooling in public."

Abby turned back toward the building's side entrance. Erin shook her head as if clearing it of confusion, then fell in step beside her.

"So why didn't you ever mention how handsome he was?" Erin asked.

"There was no point in bringing it up."

Abby opened the door. Erin went in first, waiting for Abby on the other side of the threshold. "Honey, with a man that good-looking, there's always a point. At least I would've understood why you agreed to tutor Kitty."

"It had nothing to do with him."

"Uh-huh. If you say so."

"He's a parent," Abby insisted, using the patient tone she'd use with one of her students. "That makes him off-limits."

"But he's a single parent," Erin replied in the same, patient tone, "and the school year is almost over, which makes him almost available. When was the last time you had a date?"

Abby cut across the multipurpose room, walking fast. "Don't start, Erin. I've got my future planned."

"Plans can be changed," Erin said. "Especially *some* plans." Abby opened her mouth to argue, but Erin peeled off toward her daughter's sixth-grade classroom with a cheery wave. "Later, Ab. Be sure to introduce me to Mr. Granger. For professional purposes only, of course."

"Oh, of course." Abby rolled her eyes, then hurried on to her own room. The bell went off with its usual deafening clamor, and the halls filled with excited, boisterous children and beleaguered parents, many of whom looked as if they cheerfully might kill for one more cup of coffee. Abby greeted them all— the children with hugs, the parents with sympathetic smiles.

The Grangers were the last to arrive at her door. Proudly clinging to her daddy's hand, Kitty gave Abby a shy grin.

"Hi, Ms. Walsh," she said.

"Good morning, Kitty," Abby said. "It's nice to see you here, Mr. Granger."

"Good morning, Ms. Walsh." His wry smile reminded her that she hadn't given him any choice in the matter. He offered his hand, as if to show her he held no grudges. When she laid her palm across his and he gently curled his fingers around hers, she experienced a jolt of connection that went far beyond a handshake.

Her eyes met his, and his fingers tightened imperceptibly, telling her that he'd felt it, too. A part of her wanted to explore this attraction that showed no sign of dissipating the way it should have done. But another part of her, a sadder and wiser part, flashed neon warning signals.

She'd had these feelings for a man before. She'd acted on them against her mother's most fervent advice. And she'd paid dearly for doing so. Some people simply were meant to remain single, and she firmly believed she was one of them.

It was fine to enjoy whatever time she could have with Kitty, but she couldn't start harboring romantic notions about Kitty's father, no matter how tempted she was.

Yanking her hand away so quickly that Jack stared at her in surprise, she stepped back and inclined her head toward the doorway. "It's time to get started."

He followed Kitty into the classroom without a word of protest. After she took roll, they all trooped outside to join the rest of the school at the soccer field. Abby felt Jack's thoughtful gaze frequently resting on her during the morning's activities. Bruce Watson, the P.E. teacher, introduced goofy races, relays and games that allowed everyone to participate. The kids especially enjoyed the Raw Egg Relay and the Water Balloon Blanket Toss.

Busying herself with organizing relay teams and handing out equipment, Abby managed to avoid speaking to Jack until it was almost time for lunch.

Since the play day officially would end after the picnic, she allowed herself to relax.

Big mistake.

Mr. Watson blew his whistle and raised both hands above his head. "No Mountain View Play Day would be complete without a special event for adults. Boys and girls in each class huddle up and choose two adults to represent you."

Abby watched with fond amusement while her students formed their huddle and carried on a spirited discussion, punctuated with giggles, whispers and sneaky glances in her direction. Resigned to being one of the "chosen," she studied the kids for clues to the identity of the other "lucky" adult. At first she thought her teammate would be one of her regular classroom volunteers, Brenda Munson or Mary Alice Jones.

Then, with a sinking sensation in the pit of her stomach, she saw four of her boys turn at the same time and look directly at Jack. Well, didn't that just make perfect sense? These events were designed to be highly entertaining for the kids, which automatically meant they would be as undignified and embarrassing as possible for the evil P.E. teacher's adult victims.

Pairing her up with Jack Granger virtually guaranteed an uncomfortable experience for her, no matter what this year's event turned out to be.

The kids broke out of their huddle and formed two smaller groups based on gender. In seconds, the girls surrounded Abby and gleefully escorted her to the starting line, while the boys did the same to Jack. She stood next to him, her stomach clenching, her palms sweaty, feeling all of fifteen years old again and fearing she would pass out from nerves before she actually touched the boy who'd asked her to dance.

Fortunately, Jack looked even more uneasy than she felt, which made her feel a little better about the situation. This was her turf, after all, and she had a better idea of what was liable to happen than he did. At the very least, she knew she wouldn't be the only one who wound up looking foolish.

Mr. Watson blew his whistle again. "All right, listen up now. Our special event for adults this year is—" he paused for dramatic effect "—a three-legged race!"

The crowd laughed and applauded. Abby looked up at Jack, squinting against the bright sunshine. "This could get ugly. How's your sense of humor today?"

He grinned. "Just let me lead, and we'll be fine."

Before she could think of an appropriately pithy reply, Mr. Watson handed out strips of cloth. Chuckling, Brenda Munson knelt in front of Abby and Jack, and tied Abby's right leg to Jack's left one. Abby put her right arm around Jack's waist to keep her balance.

He slid his arm across her back, hesitating as if he wasn't quite sure what to do with his hand. After a few seconds, he clamped it onto her hip and firmly pulled her against his side. The forced intimacy with him was every bit as terrible and exciting and…well, *arousing,* as she'd feared it might be.

His body heat seeped through his clothes and hers, and she could pick out the distinctive scents of his soap and his aftershave. She heard every breath he took. Felt every shift of his body, the flex and play of the muscles around his waist and torso beneath her hand.

As if the inherent awkwardness of the differences in their heights hadn't already drawn everyone's attention, Bruce Watson pointed at them and shouted, "My bet's on this pair right over here."

"You'll pay for this, Watson," Abby retorted with a fierce glare, staged partly, but not entirely, for the children's benefit.

He jumped back, fluttering nervous hands around his head. "Ooh, I'm so scared, Ms. Walsh. Please, don't hurt me."

The kids shrieked with laughter. When they finally quieted down again, Mr. Watson raised his hands and shouted, "Ready. Set. Go!"

Abby stepped off with her left foot. Jack stepped off with his right, and with his longer stride they already were in trouble.

"Wait," Abby yelped, frantically reaching to get her left arm around his waist for more support. Her fingers clutched at his belt buckle and slid away before she could get a decent grip on anything.

"We'll lose." Jack raised his left foot, which, of course, raised Abby's right one. He took a huge step, his superior strength dragging her along like a floppy puppet.

Praying she wouldn't grab anything embarrassing, Abby swung her left arm toward his waist again, her fingers groping for a belt loop, finally latching onto one. "I don't care if we lose."

"Well, I do. Hang on."

Oh, God, please save her from competitive males. Jack lunged ahead, and the crowd went nuts. Knowing they must look absolutely ridiculous, Abby let the laughter and catcalls bounce off her and gave up trying to "run" with Jack. She concentrated instead on staying upright and keeping her left foot completely off the ground.

"That's it," he said with a laugh. "Let me do all the work."

"I'd help if you wouldn't take giant steps," she grumbled.

"You're helping," he assured her.

"Yeah, right."

"Staying out of the way is helping." His breathing sounded labored.

"Are you all right?" she asked.

"Fine."

He didn't sound fine. In fact, now he was gasping for air. And no wonder, since he was dragging her along like a hundred-pound monkey clinging to his side. She watched for exactly the right moment to lower her left foot to the ground so she could help him again. The first step wasn't too bad.

But the second one was a doozy.

When her shifting weight pulled him slightly off balance, he compensated by leaning to the right. His left hand slid from her hip to her waist, and then all the way up her side until his fingers lodged under her bra band. She couldn't help a jerk of surprise. Or maybe that was *his* reaction.

It really didn't matter who'd started it. Within seconds, both of her feet left the ground, and she felt that giddy, flying-in-slow-motion sensation that comes before a spectacular fall. Jack muttered a rude word that would have made her laugh if she hadn't hit the grass with enough force to rattle her teeth, her bones and every other part of her anatomy.

Then he landed on top of her, trapping her arms

and driving out what little air she'd managed to keep in her lungs.

Some people might have found this situation sexy. Abby felt like a bug smashed on a windshield. She heard screaming all around her and desperately wanted to join in, if only to beg for oxygen. Good Lord, why didn't someone come and haul this big lug off her? Or were they all going to just stand there laughing their silly heads off while she suffocated under the dead weight of an assistant county prosecutor?

Wouldn't *that* make an interesting teaser for the local TV stations? *Prosecutor squashes first-grade teacher. Film at five.*

Groaning at the force of the impact, Jack pushed himself up onto one elbow and looked down into Abby's big green eyes. Abby's big, green, protruding eyes. Abby's big, green, protruding, *terrified* eyes? She thrashed her head back and forth, then tried to raise her shoulders, but couldn't. Her lips were turning an alarming shade of blue.

Jeez, she couldn't breathe. Must have had the wind knocked out of her.

He started to roll off her, but got tangled up in the cloth strips holding their legs together. The knots held so firm, he suspected the mom who had tied them must have done a stint as a Scout leader. By rolling in the other direction, he managed to flip onto his back, but he didn't hear her inhale.

Shoving his left hand under her shoulders, he pulled her into a sitting position. "Abby, take a breath. Come on, you can do it."

She made a gasping, squeaky little noise. He raised her right arm over her head. "Breathe, Abby. You're okay. It'll come."

Choking and sputtering, she yanked her arm out of his grasp. She pressed her palms against her chest, and he watched her closely, wishing he could breathe for her. He thumped her back with the heel of his hand, releasing a sigh of relief when she finally managed to gulp some air and her normal color gradually returned.

"All right now?" he asked.

Nodding, she gave him a wobbly smile. "Can you—" Her voice had a rough, strangled quality. She cleared her throat and tried again. "Untie us?"

"Oh. Sure." Feeling foolish for not having thought of it himself, he reached for the first strip of cloth. It was fastened just above his knee and halfway up Abby's thigh. Sometime during their brief run or their awkward fall, the knots had tightened into hard, compacted lumps.

He dug at them with his fingers, but the only thing he accomplished was to move the strip around without budging the knots. Scooting toward Abby until they were hip to hip, he created a little space between the cloth and their legs. She flinched when he dug at the knots again.

"Are you hurt?" he asked.

"No," she said, her face turning red, "just... ticklish."

Glancing down, he realized his fingertips had strayed into the personal territory around her inner thigh. He jerked his hand away and felt heat flood into his own face. "Sorry."

Kitty suddenly appeared at his side and gave him a perplexed frown. "Don't just sit there, Daddy. You're losing."

He smiled at her, but it felt pretty weak. "Well, that happens, Kitten. We fell down and—"

"So did lots of other people, but they're still going."

"They are?" He swiveled his head toward the finish line and saw that Kitty was right. The other teams were either on the ground or staggering dangerously. With a little luck, they could win. Automatically bending his right leg, he looked at Abby.

Her baleful stare stopped him cold. It was a teacher thing, of course. It annoyed him to realize that at thirty-six, he still responded to it as automatically as any six-year-old.

Kitty tugged at his arm. "Come *on,* Daddy."

"I don't think so, honey. I fell on Ms. Walsh, and she hasn't quite recovered yet."

"Are you hurt, Ms. Walsh?" Kitty asked, clearly aghast at the possibility.

Smiling, Abby shook her head. "Nothing but my dignity. Do you know Mrs. Anderson, Kitty? She works in the office?"

Kitty nodded vigorously and pointed to the sidelines. "That lady in the green shorts?"

"That's right," Abby said. "Could you run over there and tell her that we're going to need a pair of scissors?"

Kitty took off as if she'd been launched from a slingshot. Jack looked at Abby in amazement. "How do you do that?"

"Do what?" she asked.

"I have to push and prod her into everything. How do you get such immediate cooperation?"

Abby shrugged. "Most kids this age adore their teacher, and we find a way to praise them for everything they do, even if it's only a little bit right. It's a powerful motivator.''

Before he could think of an appropriate reply, Kitty and Mrs. Anderson returned, hauling an enormous denim purse. The woman had short, curly red hair, a friendly face and the presence and organizing power of a military general. He remembered her well from the day he'd registered Kitty for kindergarten.

The woman leaned over Abby. ''What's up?''

Abby waved a hand over their joined legs. ''We can't untie the knots.''

Mrs. Anderson cast a considering look at Jack. Merry blue eyes glinting with amusement, she turned back to Abby. ''You're sure you want to?''

''Yes,'' Abby hissed at her. ''Get these things off us *now*.''

Giggling, the other woman rummaged around in the depths of her purse, finally pulling out a wicked-looking pair of scissors. ''Yes, ma'am, Ms. Walsh, ma'am. Anything you say, ma'am.''

''Oh, stop,'' Abby grumbled, a smile teasing at the edges of her mouth.

A shout went up from the end of the field. Mrs. Anderson glanced up, announced, ''Mr. Everhard's room just won,'' and turned back to the job at hand. With four efficient snips, the cloth strips fell away. ''All done.''

''Thanks.'' Abby scrambled to her feet, gasped and toppled over sideways toward Jack's lap.

Seeing her face go white, he grabbed her elbow and got to his knees. ''What's wrong, Abby?''

Mrs. Anderson shot him a surprised glance, muttering, ''It's Abby now, is it?''

Abby grimaced and put her foot on the ground.

"My foot fell asleep. Oh, oh, oh, I hate that tingling sensation."

Relieved that she wasn't injured, Jack climbed to his feet, put one arm behind her knees, the other behind her shoulders and scooped her up against his chest.

"What are you doing?" she yelped.

"I believe it's called getting you off the field." He smiled and winked at Kitty, who was trotting along beside him.

"For pity's sake, I can walk," she said. "Put me down."

"I will when we get someplace you can sit down."

"I don't need to sit down."

"Sure you do. And it's no trouble for me to carry you," he said, grinning in spite of the glare she was giving him. Though he was too smart to tell her so, carrying her like this made him feel big and strong. The dramatic sighs and thumbs-ups coming from the women on the sidelines didn't hurt his ego, either.

"Mr. Granger—"

"No wonder you get along with those little kids so well. You're not much bigger than they are."

"Put me down this instant." She dug her elbow into his chest, but it didn't hurt.

"I can't." He nodded toward the group of kids charging toward them. "You'll be killed in that stampede."

The children from Abby's class gathered around him, some of them jumping like excited puppies, their voices creating a wall of sound. He finally set Abby on her feet and enjoyed watching her patiently but firmly deal with her students. Within minutes, she had them all sorted out and ready for the picnic.

He and Kitty went through the food line together. When they started looking for a place to sit, Abby waved to get his attention, then beckoned for them to join her and an attractive brunette woman sitting on a blanket. Kitty hurried over, her little face glowing when Abby greeted her with a one-armed hug.

Jack arrived at the blanket just in time to hear Abby make the introductions. "Erin, this is Kitty Granger. Kitty, this is my very best friend since the third grade, Dr. Johnson."

Kitty responded to Dr. Johnson's friendly smile with a shy smile of her own. She quickly shook hands with the brunette and snuggled closer to Abby's side. Jack set his plate on the blanket, and Abby introduced him to Dr. Johnson, as well.

Kitty's first appointment with the woman was scheduled for tomorrow. While he didn't particularly appreciate having this meeting sprung on him, Jack had to admit that it was easier on Kitty to meet Dr. Johnson in this relaxed setting and with Abby to lend her support than it would have been in an office. After a few minutes of chitchat, it was easy to see why Abby had recommended her friend to help Kitty.

Besides a ready, generous smile, Erin Johnson had lively, intelligent blue eyes that reflected her genuine interest in whomever she was talking with. It was an engaging trait—one, he suspected, that would make it extremely easy to confide in her. Kitty certainly took to her in a hurry.

Halfway through her hamburger, Kitty leaned close to Abby and whispered something. Abby smiled at her, then wrinkled her forehead as if she were thinking very hard.

"Well, sweetie, I'm supposed to stay out here to

help supervise the children, but I'll bet Dr. Johnson would take you to the bathroom.''

"Oh, sure, I'd be glad to." Dr. Johnson scrambled to her feet, held out one hand to Kitty and looked at Jack. "That is, I'd be glad to if it's okay with your daddy."

Kitty turned to him, practically dancing from one foot to the other. "Is it okay?"

"Go ahead, Kitten, it's fine," he said.

She put her hand in Dr. Johnson's, and the two of them headed for the building, gabbing like old friends. When they were out of earshot, Jack looked at Abby. "Why didn't you warn me I was going to meet her today?"

"Erin didn't want me to," Abby said with a rueful smile. "She thought you might be uptight about meeting her, and that Kitty would pick up on your tension."

"That's a possibility," he admitted.

"So, what do you think of her so far?"

"Kitty sure likes her."

"That's not what I asked. What do *you* think of her?"

"She seems...nice," Jack answered. "She inspires confidence."

Abby's smile of approval warmed his heart. "I was hoping you'd feel that way. I'm hardly impartial, but I honestly believe that if anybody can help Kitty, Erin can."

Jack nodded thoughtfully. "I appreciate your recommendation. Kitty's going to her first appointment tomorrow afternoon. She'll miss the last hour of school."

"Fine. I'll send home the work sheets she'll miss.

Will you call and let me know how the appointment goes?''

''Sure. Who knows? I may need advice or a shoulder to cry on.''

Abby chuckled softly, then turned her head away as if she'd heard something important. Jack looked off in the same direction, and saw Kitty and Dr. Johnson skipping down the sidewalk on their way back to the blanket. He grinned at the picture they made, until Kitty tripped and fell on her hands and knees on the concrete. Dr. Johnson squatted down beside her, while Jack and Abby scrambled to their feet.

Before they could even step off the blanket, Kitty got up and ran toward them, tears raining down her face and a thin trickle of blood oozing down her leg from a cut on her knee. Jack opened his arms to catch her, but she ran to Abby. He handed Abby a paper napkin he hadn't used.

She used it to wipe Kitty's shin while keeping up a steady stream of cheerful chatter that stopped Kitty's tears and eventually made her laugh. Dr. Johnson flagged down the school nurse, who brought over a first-aid kit.

Jack watched the women working on his daughter, feeling bemused and left out. Kitty didn't even notice that he wasn't in the huddle with her. She was too busy basking in all that attention. Especially Abby's.

Abby's arm curved protectively around Kitty's shoulders. Kitty leaned against Abby's side as if she had every right to do so. From the way they naturally tipped their heads together, anyone observing them from a distance would be excused for thinking they were mother and daughter, in spite of the difference in their hair color.

His chest tightened and his breath caught in his lungs. Here was indisputable proof that he'd been right when he'd decided that Abby was the solution to Kitty's problems. And his own. Every time he saw her, he liked her more. Eventually he *would* marry her—but first, he had to convince her to go out on a date with him.

He went straight home after the picnic, planted the last of the flowers and waited until he'd put Kitty to bed that night. Then he went downstairs to his den, dialed Abby's number and sat back with his feet braced on a corner of the desk, his heart beating faster with each ring.

Three rings later, she answered. "Hello. Abby Walsh speaking."

"Hi, Abby, it's Jack Granger."

"Oh, dear, is Kitty crying again?"

He smiled at the instant concern in her voice. "She's fine. Sound asleep, in fact."

"Is everything all right?"

"I just wanted to talk to you." He felt foolish admitting that, especially when there was a long, silent pause on Abby's end of the line.

"What did you want to talk about?" she finally asked.

"It was a nice picnic today. I'm glad you pushed me to be there."

"You said you were planning to be there, anyway."

He shrugged, then remembered she couldn't see him. "I was, but it turned out to be even better than I expected. You told Kitty you and Dr. Johnson have been friends since the third grade. Did you have something to do with Kitty getting such an early appointment with her?"

"Hey, what are friends for?" Abby said with a laugh.

"I really appreciate it, Abby."

"It's my pleasure. I'm pretty fond of your little girl."

"She feels the same about you. Talks about you all the time."

"That must get old."

"Not at all," he said. "In fact, that's why I'm calling. I'd like to get better acquainted with you. Would you have dinner with me on Saturday night?"

There was another long pause. Suddenly feeling incredibly nervous, he realized he actually was holding his breath.

"It's a lovely invitation, but I can't accept it," she said, her voice soft. "I don't date the parents of my students."

"Well, it doesn't really have to be a date, exactly," he said, backpedaling like crazy. Good thing he was so much smoother in court, or he'd lose every case.

He heard a smile in her voice when she replied. "What else would you call having dinner on a Saturday night?"

"Well, it's just a token of my gratitude for all the help you've given to Kitty this year."

"That's really not necessary."

"Maybe not necessary, but it might be fun. Don't you think?"

"I think I'm sticking with my policy. I don't date my students' parents."

"Then, we'll wait until school gets out. Next Thursday, right?"

"That's the last day, yes. But—"

"So, let's go out this weekend, and you can celebrate the start of your summer vacation. It'll just be a casual evening out. If it makes you feel better, we'll even talk about Kitty's tutoring schedule."

"Well, all right," she said after yet another long silence.

Her hesitation was hardly flattering, but he supposed he deserved it. Still, he'd gotten this far. He was confident that once they got to know each other and she had more chances to bond with Kitty, her resistance to him would fade.

"Great," he said. "I'll be in touch to set a time."

"Good luck tomorrow at Kitty's appointment."

"I'll call you after school and tell you about it."

They said good-night. Jack hung up the phone, then sat back again, making a mental list of the local restaurants Abby might enjoy. He'd approach wooing her with the same logic and strategy he'd use to build a case for court. It was all in the details. Get the details right, and he'd get the right results.

Chapter Seven

Abby glanced at her bedroom clock and hurriedly pulled on the clothes she'd laid out for her dinner with Jack. She wished she hadn't agreed to do this. Wished she hadn't let Erin's needling about how long it'd been since she'd had a date cloud her judgment. Wished she didn't feel so ridiculously nervous. Or so ambivalent.

Muttering, "For heaven's sake, it's just dinner," she sat on the side of her bed, poked her feet into a pair of panty hose, stood and tugged the panty part up over her hips. She shouldn't have waited so late to get ready, but she'd worked hard all day taking down bulletin boards, cleaning out her classroom and packing her file boxes and other personal belongings.

Then there'd been a farewell party for her in the teachers' lounge. By the time she'd brought home all her stuff and stored it, she'd needed a bath and a nap.

And now she was late. Not terribly late, but late enough to unsettle her.

Yanking her hot pink sundress off its hanger, she pulled it on over her head and let the soft fabric slither down her body. She slid her feet into a tall, strappy pair of sandals and hurried into the bathroom to put on makeup and beat her hair into submission.

She'd just finished putting in her earrings when Jack arrived. Taking a deep breath, she crossed the room at a leisurely pace and opened the door. Oh, goodness.

There he stood, even more handsome than usual in a gray, summer-weight suit, a blue shirt that brought out the color of his eyes and a blue-and-gray striped tie. And he was holding a bouquet of daisies.

He gave her an unhurried, appreciative once-over. "Hello, Abby."

Since her heart didn't know whether it wanted to melt or flutter at his sexy smile and the deep, caressing note in his voice, it just missed a beat. He handed her the flowers. Accepting them, she stepped back, inviting him into the apartment.

"Thank you." She buried her nose in the flowers and inhaled their rich scent. "They're wonderful. I'll go and put them in water, and then I'd better change into something a little more dressy."

"Don't," he said immediately, giving her another inspection that threw her heart into confusion all over again. "I really like that dress."

She raised her eyebrows. "You're not exactly dressed for a 'casual evening out.'"

"Forget what I'm wearing." His grin could have been teasing, but his eyes said he was absolutely serious. "You look fantastic."

How *had* she ever called this charming man Grumpface Granger? Well, he hadn't always been so charming, and she would do well to remember that. She carried the bouquet into the kitchen, excruciatingly aware that he was following her. She could practically feel his heated gaze on her behind.

The thought made her feel so self-conscious, it was a wonder she didn't trip or fall off her sandals. Though she felt like a complete fraud, she did her best to act as casual as he was acting. She stuck the flowers in a vase, filled it with water and thanked him again for bringing them.

"You're welcome." He glanced at the clock on her stove. "I made reservations for seven-thirty. Are you ready to go?"

"That depends." She led the way back to the living room. "Where are we going?"

"That's privileged information."

She frowned at him. "Are you sure I'm appropriately dressed? It'll only take a minute to change."

"You're fine, Abby." He walked to the door and opened it, then looked back at her with an expectant expression. "Trust me."

Abby picked up her purse and the silky white cardigan she'd laid out for later in the evening. "Yeah, yeah, and the check's in the mail, Granger."

He laughed, then escorted her out to his full-size sedan. Twenty minutes later he turned into the parking lot at The Flour Mill, a working mill that had ground the area's wheat for almost eighty years. Built beside the Spokane River for power, the building had been converted into restaurants and shops while keeping the original redbrick walls and hewn-wood floors intact.

Abby loved the old building's atmosphere and tried to stop in whenever she went downtown. Ever the gentleman, Jack escorted her straight to the entrance of Clinkerdagger, a popular restaurant since Spokane had hosted the World's Fair in 1974. This wasn't the kind of place she associated with a casual date, but just looking at the sign made her mouth water. When they stepped inside, the aroma of prime rib made her stomach growl.

Mortified, she glanced at Jack, wondering if he'd heard it, but he was busy talking to the maître d', thank goodness. Her budget rarely stretched enough to allow her to eat at a restaurant this expensive, but she didn't want him to think she didn't know how to behave. A moment later a waiter showed them through a walkway to a table next to a window overlooking the river's falls.

Abby sighed in appreciation. She knew how hard it was to get a falls view; she'd made reservations weeks in advance for Erin's birthday last year. The Old English decor created a relaxed, comfortable and cozy setting. She felt pampered even to be here, and Jack's solicitousness when he held her chair and asked the waiter to describe the house specialties for her before placing their drink order added to her pleasure.

He smiled at her across the table, his eyes a darker shade of blue in the candlelight. "I hope you like this place."

"What's not to like?"

Her worry about the wisdom of going out with Jack evaporated beneath the power of the wonderful food, the romantic atmosphere and his considerable charm. She quite simply enjoyed his company as they progressed from appetizers to dessert. When the waiter brought their Burnt Cream, she asked Jack a question she'd wanted to raise ever since she'd met him.

"Why did you become a prosecutor? Why not a defense attorney or a corporate attorney?"

He gave her a partial shrug. "My standard answer is that it was the first job I got when I graduated from law school, and I liked it so much I never left."

"Then, what's the *real* answer?"

"My brother Dan thinks it has something to do with our dad's murder."

"I'm so sorry. I didn't mean to bring up a painful topic."

"Relax, it happened a long time ago and there's no reason you should've remembered it," he said with a wry smile. "You were just a kid."

"Do you mind telling me what happened?"

Jack took a sip of coffee, then set down his cup. "He was a cop, like both of my brothers. One night he made a routine traffic stop and was shot. He died at the scene, and the case was never solved."

"How old were you?"

"Twelve. Suddenly, I was the man of the house."

"That's a huge burden for a child."

He shrugged again, indicating that it hadn't been so bad. "My mom was pretty tough, and Dad's friends on the force stopped by fairly often and helped out as much as they could."

"But they had lives and families of their own, and you were left to help and support your mom and grow up on your own."

He frowned thoughtfully for a moment, then nodded. "That's about it. How did you know?

"I grew up without a dad, too."

"Really? Why?"

Abby stiffened. She couldn't believe she'd told Jack even that much. An all-too-familiar sense of grief and anger washed over her, robbing her of any desire to continue this conversation or finish her dessert. Pushing her dish away, she said, "I don't discuss that."

Jack's eyes widened in obvious surprise, and he studied her for a moment, his expression becoming more thoughtful. She suspected he was trying to think of a way to make her talk, but this wasn't a courtroom and she wasn't a defendant he could grill.

"Do you discuss whether or not you have any sisters and brothers?"

"I could," she said, disarmed by the cleverness of his question, "but I wouldn't have much to say."

"You're an only child?"

Abby nodded. "And no, I wasn't particularly spoiled— Did your mother remarry?"

"Are you kidding? She wouldn't even date. And believe me, she had plenty of opportunities."

"Where does she live now?"

"She's in Texas taking care of her parents. They're not that old by today's standards, but they both have severe health problems, so she feels obligated to help them."

"Otherwise, she'd be here helping you with Kitty?"

"Oh, yeah. Big time. It kills her that she doesn't get to see more of her only grandchild. Especially a girl grandchild. I think she always regretted not having a daughter."

The waiter came by and refilled their coffee cups.

Abby took a sip. "It's too bad she's missing out on Kitty's childhood. She's such a special little girl."

"Did *your* mother remarry?" Jack asked.

Abby sadly shook her head. "She wouldn't date, either. It made it hard to leave home."

"You're not from Spokane?"

Leaning forward, Abby lowered her voice. "Don't tell anybody, but I'm a…westsider."

"No! Not one of those," Jack protested with a mock grimace, his eyes glinting with laughter. "You're not actually from…Seattle. Are you?"

She demurely lowered her eyes. "I'm afraid so."

He squinted at her like an old man trying to see far into the distance. "Well, you *look* pretty normal. For a westsider, that is."

Abby laughed out loud. "Thanks. I think. You don't look *too* much like a hick. For an eastsider, that is."

"Well, at least you're not a…" He paused and shuddered, and she finished the sentence with him. *"—Californian."*

They laughed together, and the rich, intimate sound they made seemed so natural and right, it gave Abby goose bumps. She couldn't remember the last time she'd enjoyed talking with a man so much. Well, she *could,* but she didn't particularly want to, since the man in question had been her ex-husband.

Whenever Tad's name popped into her mind, all she could think about was what a fool she'd been to date him, much less marry him. He'd betrayed her trust in the cruelest way possible, and she hadn't even been tempted to have a serious relationship with anyone else. Until now.

The goose bumps came from realizing that Jack

Granger could tempt her. In many ways. On many levels.

Good thing she had her life planned for the foreseeable future. It didn't include a man or a little girl, no matter how much they might appeal to her, individually or as a pair. She had important work to do, and it was time for her to remember that.

Jack signaled for the check, while they talked about Washington's unique political issues. He watched Abby's face closely, fascinated with the myriad expressions she had, liking each one better than the last. She was intelligent, lively company. It had been a long time since he'd enjoyed an evening as much this one.

Every now and then a shadow darkened her eyes and stole the brightness of her smile. It had just happened again. He wanted to ask her what caused it, but after her abrupt withdrawal earlier, he didn't want to risk provoking another withdrawal by trespassing into personal territory.

But dammit, he wanted to know her—her background, her hopes, her dreams. He knew she was single now, but he didn't know if she'd ever been married. He wanted to know that and so many other things.

What would it be like to kiss her? What kind and color of underwear did she have on under that sexy little dress? How would it feel to make love with her?

Wow. That was quite a leap for a first date. He didn't see himself as being particularly lecherous, but his libido took notice whenever he saw Abby.

Or even thought about her.

The woman was dangerous to his peace of mind,

but he still wanted to explore this attraction he felt for her, unlikely as it seemed. He'd never been attracted to such a short woman. He normally preferred brunettes or redheads to blondes. And he'd actually disliked her for months.

But now, he really wanted to spend time with her. Was that for Kitty? Or for himself? At the moment, he couldn't separate the impulses. It didn't matter why—he just wanted to be with her.

They both were quiet during the drive back to her apartment. When he parked in the lot behind her building, she turned to him with a sweet smile.

"It was a wonderful dinner, Jack. Thank you."

"You're welcome." He stepped out of the car and rounded the hood to help her out, but she didn't wait for him. By the time he got there, she was closing the passenger door behind her.

"You don't need to come upstairs with me," she said. "I'm perfectly capable of getting to my apartment on my own."

"I know that," he said with a grin, "but humor me. My mom taught us to act like gentlemen, and her first rule was that a gentleman always sees a lady safely to her door. You don't want me to feel guilty all night, do you?"

"Oh, of course not."

She took the arm he offered, and they walked up the two flights of steps to her apartment. At her door, she turned to him, no doubt ready to thank him again. The instant she opened her mouth, he couldn't resist satisfying his curiosity on at least one count.

Lowering his head, he captured her mouth in a kiss that started out gentle and, in a matter of seconds, escalated into something far more erotic than he would have believed possible. Their lips fused. Their tongues entwined. She tasted luscious, like Burnt Cream and strong coffee and sex all wrapped up together. His body immediately hardened in response. Fearing he'd blow a circuit, he told himself to pull away, but, instead, found himself pulling her against him.

She embraced him for a moment, melted into his arms as if she were coming home. In the next heartbeat, however, she planted one palm in the center of his chest and firmly pushed him away. Shaking her head as if to clear it, she inhaled several times before looking up to meet his gaze, her eyes utterly serious.

"I can't do this, Jack."

Damn, had he misunderstood why she preferred to be called Ms. Walsh? "You're not married, are you?"

"No, I'm divorced," she said evenly. "I'm not interested in starting a relationship right now."

"Meaning?"

"I'm trying to be honest with you." She glanced away and her cheeks flushed. "I don't want to mislead you into thinking I might...well, I'm really not looking for a relationship at all right now."

"Is there a special reason?"

"Yes, I'm moving to Portland."

"*What?*" he demanded, seeing his plans going up in smoke.

"I'm moving to Portland. As in Oregon."

He wanted to rake both hands through his hair, decided he should at least try to play it cool. Propping his shoulder against the door casing, he crossed one foot over the other. "When are you leaving?"

"At the end of August." She fished a key out of her purse, then looked up at him again.

"That's why you insisted on finding a replacement tutor for Kitty by July, isn't it. And why you've been so concerned about letting her get attached to you."

"Exactly. Getting involved with you just makes the whole situation more complicated."

"Would you feel differently if you were staying in Spokane?"

She smiled. "I might." He raised an eyebrow and she chuckled. "All right. I admit it. I'm attracted to you, but I am leaving and I don't do casual sex. I just can't get involved that way."

A pair of adolescent girls passed them on the walkway, heads down, their shoulders shaking with silent laughter. When they reached the stairway, they ran down one flight of stairs and burst into a fit of giggles.

Abby muttered, "Oh, for heaven's sake," opened her door and motioned for Jack to come inside with her. "That's no place to have a private conversation."

Jack grinned. "It could've been worse. Imagine what they would've done if you'd been telling me you *did* do casual sex."

Abby laughed and shook her head. "Oh, bite your tongue. I'd have to move right now."

"If you didn't, you'd probably have lots of guys at your door trying to borrow a cup of sugar." He wandered around her living room, studying an extensive and eclectic collection of figurines, class and candid photographs of her students, little plaques with I-Love-My-Teacher sentiments and framed children's artwork.

She rolled her eyes at him. "Oh, please, flattery

will get you nowhere. Would you like some coffee or a soft drink?''

''I'm fine,'' he said, rejoining her by the sofa. ''But if it's not too personal a question, I'd like to know why you're leaving Spokane.''

They sat down together. She smoothed her skirt over her thighs, and her eyes lit up like a couple of emeralds under a bright light. ''I'm going to be a college professor. And I'm so excited about it, I can hardly wait.''

He couldn't believe what he was hearing. ''You're not going to teach little kids anymore?''

''Not on a regular basis. I'll probably do some classroom work in order to demonstrate my methods to other teachers. Why are you frowning?''

He hadn't realized he was, and did his best to stop. ''No reason, really. I mean, it's none of my business.''

''But what were you thinking?''

''It's just that you're such a good teacher. And I always thought you really enjoyed working with children.''

''I do.''

''Then why give it up?''

''Because our education system is in trouble, and I think I know at least one way to improve it.''

''Tell me about it.''

She leaned forward, her face and body radiating enthusiasm and energy for her subject. This was a woman who had a dream and the drive to make it happen.

''There have been movements afoot in education for years, trying to get teachers to work on an individual basis with each student, but that hasn't been practical in a lot of cases. We're not trained well enough, and we don't have that kind of time, so a lot of us still teach with a one-size-fits-all mentality.''

"What would you do differently?"

"At the beginning of the year, I give all of my kids a simple test that helps me pinpoint their personality types.''

"What difference does that make?''

"All the difference in the world. People with one personality type learn more easily if information is presented to them in a certain way. But that way may frustrate or confuse people with another personality type. No type is right or wrong. It's just a difference in preferences.''

"That makes sense. But how do you put it into action?''

"Once I have all of the kids tested, I can group them in the most productive way, depending on what I'm trying to accomplish. So, at the most, I only have to come up with three or four different approaches to teach a new concept instead of one for every kid in the class. And if somebody's not getting something, I can usually figure out a better approach to help that particular child, based on personality type, than just going over and over the information in the same way they didn't understand in the first place.''

"You've actually done all of this?''

"For the past four years. And it works, Jack. That's the most exciting thing about it. My students usually have great test scores in reading and in math.''

"No exceptions?''

"There are always exceptions. Some children aren't mature enough to stay on task. Some children don't have the raw intelligence to handle the material.''

"What about Kitty?''

"Oh, she's really bright. I've told you that before. She's not immature, either. She's just been disengaged from the learning process. The therapy will fix that, and then you'll be shocked at how fast she learns new things.''

"I hope you're right,'' he said with feeling. "We met with Dr. Johnson again yesterday, and last night Kitty had a nightmare and wet the bed.''

"Oh, poor baby. It sounds like it's probably going to get worse before it gets better—but don't give up.''

"I won't,'' he assured her. "Let's get back to your plans.''

"They're not very complicated. Once I finish my dissertation, I'll start preparing my lectures for the fall quarter. Then I'll go to Portland and find a place to live, and as soon as I'm moved, I'll be starting my new job.''

"Where are you going to teach?''

"It's a small, private school with a big education department. I'm really looking forward to it.''

"I can see that. But won't you miss the kids?''

"Probably,'' she admitted with a smile tinged with sadness. "It's always a joy to see them get excited when they conquer some new concept. And children are so honest about their feelings. I love that about them.''

"But you're still willing to give it up?''

"I need to. This is bigger than me or my career. It's a chance to make a real difference for kids all over the country. Now do you understand why I can't get involved? It really isn't personal, Jack.''

"I understand that," he said. "But this sounds like a long-term mission. Don't you want to remarry and have a family someday?"

"No, I'm already married to my work."

Her answer sounded firm, but somehow automatic. As if she'd given it many times before. The sadness he'd seen earlier flashed in her eyes, quick and sharp. It faded just as quickly, making him wonder if he'd imagined it. He didn't think so. And what had happened to end her marriage? He didn't dare ask, but he sure wanted to.

"What?" she asked, making him realize he hadn't responded to her statement. "You look like you don't believe me."

"It's not that," he protested. "All of this is a big surprise. You're so warm and loving with Kitty and the rest of your class, I can't get my mind around the idea of your never having children of your own."

She stiffened up as if someone had poured cement into her spine. "Not every woman is meant to be a wife and mother."

"You think you're one of them?"

"I know I am." Her voice took on a warning edge. "Can we drop this subject now?"

"Of course. And I appreciate your honesty, believe me."

"But…" she prompted. "I hear a definite 'but' at the end of your sentence. You might as well finish it."

"All right. *But* I'd still like to go out with you."

"Oh, Jack—"

"Hear me out before you say no." He paused, waiting until she relented enough to nod at him. "I haven't dated anyone since Gina died. It's felt nice to be around a woman again. I really enjoyed being out with you, Abby. A lot.''

"What are you trying to say?"

"I'm rusty at this dating thing. I just thought, you know, since you've put your cards on the table and we both know what's *not* going to happen, maybe you'd be willing to help me get back in the swing. I'm just talking about casual dates. Between friends. Please?''

It took her so long to answer, he didn't know what to think. But finally, she gave him a wry smile and a nod.

"All right. As long as we have an understanding."

"No problem." Fearing she might change her mind if he stayed, Jack made a show of looking at his watch. "Well, I'd better get home and see how Kitty's doing."

Abby walked him to the door. "Thanks again for the flowers and dinner."

"You're welcome. You'll be over on Monday to tutor Kitty?"

"I'll be there. You can count on it."

He drove home, her last sentence repeating itself in his mind. He'd count on that, and a lot more. He admired Abby's ambition and honestly wanted to see her accomplish her goals. But she didn't have to go to Portland to do that.

Spokane had three four-year colleges within easy driving distance, each with an education department. It might take her a while to find a job at one of those schools, of course. But if he could convince her that she loved him and Kitty enough, she might be willing to stay in Spokane with them until she found one.

If not, he was confident they could work out an

acceptable compromise. He certainly wasn't ready to give up on his plan to marry her. As long as he could continue to see her and keep her engaged with Kitty, there was hope.

couldn't believe how easily he'd bought her explanations.

And just why *had* he bought them so easily? She couldn't figure that out at all. He seemed like a man who didn't give up when he really wanted something. So maybe he hadn't really wanted her that much. Oh, yes, he had. She'd *felt* the evidence. So to speak.

Now that she thought about it, the least he could have done was try to kiss her again. But oh, no, he'd been Mr. Perfect Gentleman, and she really should respect him for that, be grateful to him for backing off so quickly.

But she wasn't grateful. Not really. Not even a little bit. She'd wanted to kiss him again. She still did.

"You are simply perverse, Abigail," she said, using the intonation her mother used when she was seriously peeved at her.

"Yeah, tell me all about it, Mom."

Oh, brother. She was actually holding an imaginary conversation with her mother, who was in Seattle. Was that proof enough that men made women crazy, or what? Time for a reality check.

If the prospect of seeing Jack again made her pulse run fast, it was no big deal. He was a decent, good-looking man in his prime. She was a healthy, young woman. It was perfectly natural for her to feel sexually attracted to him, but her relationship with him didn't have to be complicated. She could and would tutor Kitty while maintaining a reasonable, professional distance from both of them. End of argument.

Inhaling another deep breath of the sweet country air, Abby rang the doorbell. She looked around the yard while she waited for someone to answer, noting that Jack had managed to find time to plant the flowers he'd bought. The flower beds on either side of the steps now held a colorful array of petunias and pansies.

"Hello?"

Whirling around, Abby found herself facing a stocky, white-haired woman wearing blue polyester pants and a short-sleeved camp shirt in an unfortunate shade of brown. Her short hair frizzed around her chubby face and her mouth turned upward at the corners, the wrinkles radiating from them suggesting that a smile was her normal expression.

Her eyes raked Abby from head to toe in a heartbeat. She might smile often, but she was nobody's fool.

"What can I do for you, dear?" she asked.

"My name is Abby Walsh. I'll be tutoring Kitty this summer."

"Oh, yes, you're the teacher." The woman unlatched the screen door and held it open. "I'm so pleased to meet you. Jack said you'd be here today. Come on in."

"Thank you." Abby stepped inside.

The older woman held out her hand. "I'm Millie Patten. I look after the house and Kitty."

Abby shook hands with her, wondering why she had put the house ahead of Kitty, but before she could say anything, Millie turned toward the living room and called, "Kitty! Come here, honey."

A moment later a wan-looking Kitty appeared in the doorway. Her eyes widened when she saw Abby. "Hi, Ms. Walsh. Did you come to visit me again?"

Millie stroked Kitty's hair with affection and said to Abby, "I've got to see to supper now. You just go on ahead and do whatever you need to do. Let me know if you want something.''

''Thank you,'' Abby said again, but the woman already was halfway to the kitchen. Mentally shaking her head, Abby crouched down to talk to Kitty. ''So how do you like summer vacation so far?''

''It's okay,'' Kitty said without much enthusiasm. ''You want to see my bedroom?''

''I already did once,'' Abby pointed out.

''Yeah, but I didn't get to show you my stuff,'' Kitty said solemnly.

''That's right. We were busy with other things.'' Abby smiled and held out her hand. ''All right, then, we'd better take another look.''

Kitty slid her hand into Abby's and accompanied her up the stairs. The same perfect hand that had decorated the kitchen had been at work in Kitty's bedroom. It was painted a soft shade of lavender. There were frilly white curtains at the window and a thick, multicolored carpet on the floor. A quilt with a bunny pattern and a matching pillow sham covered the bed. The window sported a window seat cushioned with a pad made from the same material.

An assortment of educational toys, books and games was so neatly stacked on a set of shelves, Abby suspected they rarely were used. A small red suitcase sat on the child-size table. Kitty opened it to reveal a handful of pretty rocks, a shiny blackbird's feather, a pink barrette, a pair of purple sunglasses and a postcard from the Statue of Liberty.

Sitting on the end of the bed, Abby admired each small treasure in turn, asking questions and watching Kitty drink in her attention like a parched plant soaking up water. And no wonder. If the busy housekeeper—who did more housekeeping than baby-sitting—and her reticent daddy were the main people in Kitty's daily life, the poor child must be starved for conversation.

While Kitty had a lot of "stuff" to show her, the one thing Abby expected to see wasn't there. She'd been too busy comforting the child the last time she'd been here to notice there were no pictures of Kitty's mother in her room. Today the omission seemed startling.

"I understand you've been visiting my friend Dr. Johnson," Abby said, her tone as casual as she could make it.

Twining her fingers together, Kitty looked down at them. "I don't like to go there."

"Why not, sweetie? Dr. Johnson's a nice lady, and the last time I saw her office, she had lots of neat toys to play with."

One skinny little shoulder rose in a halfhearted shrug. "I don't like to talk about some things."

"What kind of things?"

"Just things. Makes me feel bad."

"Oh, I see," Abby murmured. "You know, I've talked to people like Dr. Johnson about things that made me feel bad."

Kitty looked up, eyebrows arched in surprise. "You have?"

Abby nodded. "Uh-huh. I talked to a psychologist one time when I was really, really sad. I didn't like it much at first, either—but you know what?"

"What?"

"After a few visits, I started to feel better."

"Really?" Kitty's voice was filled with doubt, but her eyes held a spark of what looked like hope.

"Really," Abby assured her. "The more I talked about what was making me sad, the better I felt. And then one day, I didn't feel sad anymore, so I didn't need to go back again."

"How many visits did it take?"

"I don't remember exactly, but it was probably at least ten. Maybe twelve."

Kitty's face fell, and she let out a sigh that sounded as if it had come all the way up from her toenails. "That many?"

If ever a child needed a hug, Kitty did. Abby opened her arms, smiling to herself when Kitty climbed onto her lap and rested her head on Abby's breasts without the slightest hesitation.

For years Abby had yearned for moments of closeness like this with a child of her own. Cuddling this little girl filled an aching, empty spot near the center of Abby's heart. She stroked Kitty's soft hair with one hand and rubbed her back with the other. "It's different for everyone, honey. You might need fewer visits. You might need more. The important thing is for you to start feeling better."

"I don't think that will ever happen," Kitty whispered, her eyes filling with tears.

"Oh, I do," Abby said softly. "Dr. Johnson is very good at helping children. She's helped five of my students just in the past two years. If you'll give her a chance, I'll bet she can fix you right up."

"Other kids feel bad, too?"

"Sure they do," Abby said. "Everybody does, sometimes. You didn't think you were the only one, did you?"

Kitty nodded vigorously. Abby smoothed her hair down and rocked her back and forth, murmuring reassurances until the little girl relaxed. By the time Kitty voluntarily slid off her lap and seemed ready to move on to something else, they should have been finishing the tutoring session instead of getting ready to start it.

It didn't matter. Kitty had needed comforting and encouragement, and Abby had been glad to provide both.

She had no idea how much Jack had told Kitty about the plan to help her catch up with her classmates, but decided this would be a good time to open the subject. She moved down to the floor, sat with her feet crossed Indian-style and patted the carpet beside her.

"Come and sit down, Kitty. I want to talk to you about something."

Kitty did so, mimicking Abby's posture and position. "What is it?"

"I know you had a hard time at school the past few months. It wasn't easy for you to keep up with the rest of the class," Abby said gently. "Was it?"

Kitty lowered her head, hunched her shoulders up around her neck and twisted her fingers together in her lap. "I didn't mean to," she mumbled.

"I know, sweetie. It's all right."

The little girl raised her head and looked at Abby, her forehead wrinkled with anxiety. "If I try harder next year, will I be able to go to second grade?"

Abby brushed a strand of hair out of Kitty's face, then tucked a couple of fingers under her chin. "That's why I came here today."

"Really?"

"Yes, ma'am. Your daddy and I talked about it, and I'm going to be meeting with you for a while during your summer vacation, so you can get caught up. Will that be all right with you?''

Kitty nodded, slowly at first, and then with a genuine eagerness that convinced Abby she'd made the right decision in agreeing to tutor this child, whatever price she might have to pay later on.

''Just you and me?''

''That's right. Shall we get started?''

''Yeah,'' Kitty said.

Five minutes later, Abby had her ensconced at the dining room table with a phonics workbook and a box of crayons. Kitty worked diligently for ten minutes, and when her attention began to wander, Abby switched to flash cards with simple arithmetic problems. They had a delightful rhythm going, when Millie came into the room, car keys in one hand and a voluminous purse in the other.

''I'm so sorry to bother you, but I've got somewhere I've really got to be in ten minutes. Do you think you could stay with Kitty until Mr. Granger gets home?''

''Excuse me?'' Abby said. ''Shouldn't you ask *him?*''

''Oh, I'm sure he won't mind.'' Millie chortled and waved her keys around. ''He must trust you or he wouldn't have hired you to tutor Kitty, don't you know? He's supposed to be here at six—it's already twenty-five after, and I just can't wait for him any longer. Will you stay with her?''

''But—''

Kitty broke in, her voice filled with distress. ''Don't you want to be with me anymore, Ms. Walsh?''

''Oh, sweetie, of course I do. It's just that—''

"Well, that's fine, then. There's no need for both of us to hang around here cooling our heels." Millie came over to the table and gave Kitty a quick hug. "I'll see you tomorrow, little one."

She was out the door before Abby could so much as blink. Abby stared after the housekeeper for a moment, then turned to Kitty. "My goodness. I can't believe she did that."

The little girl shrugged, then made a funny, scrunched-up face. "Millie's weird sometimes."

"She doesn't leave you alone, does she?"

"No," Kitty said. "Sometimes she's kinda bossy, but mostly she's okay."

Abby didn't know whether to laugh or cry at Kitty's matter-of-fact assessment of Millie's personality, but she intended to tell Jack about it as soon as he got home. Whenever that was.

Praying a cop wouldn't catch him, Jack sped home. He'd been trying so hard to get home on time—damn his boss for calling him in for a last-minute briefing and making him late. Millie would get on his case again, and he was anxious to find out how Kitty's first tutoring session had gone. His stomach acid churned higher with every mile.

By the time he parked in the drive beside Abby's Bronco, he had a headache to match his heartburn. That was odd. Millie's station wagon was gone, and he hadn't expected Abby to be here this late. What in the world was happening now? Worried, he grabbed his briefcase and jogged to the house, bracing himself.

The first sound he heard when he opened the back door was laughter. He paused, allowing himself to savor that sound for a moment. How bad could it be, if Abby and Kitty were laughing?

Looking across the kitchen, he encountered a scene so unexpectedly sweet, so touching, that he felt as if his brother had just slugged him. He rocked back on his heels and shook his head to make sure he wasn't imagining it. But when he looked again, they were still there.

Heads close together, Abby and Kitty stood on opposite sides of the work island, Kitty on a step stool, the open peanut butter jar sitting in front of her. She held a table knife in one hand and a celery stick in the other. Her little tongue sticking out the side of her mouth in intense concentration, she carefully drew the knife across the celery stick, looking to Abby for approval when she reached the other end.

"Good job, sweetie," Abby crowed, her bright, delighted smile filling the room.

Her face glowing, Kitty giggled, then licked peanut butter off her index finger.

Oh, God, it used to be like this. He'd drag his tired butt home from a tough day at work, walk into this house and find a happy child and a warm, sexy woman waiting for him. The irritations of his job would fall away, and he suddenly would remember what a lucky man he was. This was a different time and a different woman, but it didn't matter one bit.

Everything about this moment, this scene felt right. Abby belonged with Kitty and with him. Not just because they needed her or because she could solve his problems; it went deeper than that. She really belonged with them.

He just knew it.

At work he dealt so much in provable facts and

physical evidence, he rarely paid attention to flashes of intuition. But this one about Abby was so strong, he couldn't dismiss it. Didn't even want to dismiss it, and it felt okay.

He would never stop loving Gina, but he was glad to realize that now he could get on with his life. Glad to find himself ready to let his grief pass and start living again. And glad—fiercely glad—that his libido finally had decided to wake up. He wasn't ready— well, Abby wasn't ready—to do anything about it, but his life had been damn dull without it.

He set his briefcase on the floor beside the back door and slowly crossed the room, absently noting a skillet and a cooking pot sitting on the stove. "Hello, ladies."

Kitty looked up and grinned at him, showing off the gap where her adult front teeth were growing in. "Hi, Daddy. We're cooking supper."

"Great. What are you making?"

"Ms. Walsh is making tortilla soup and grilled cheese samwiches. An' I'm making ants on a log."

Smiling at the pride in Kitty's voice, Jack looked over her shoulder at a plate filled with peanut butter-stuffed celery sticks, each topped with a line of raisins. He pointed at a raisin. "Are those the ants?"

Kitty nodded vigorously, then picked up one of the "logs" and offered it to him. "Want one?"

"Thanks." He accepted the celery stick, biting off the end well beyond the first "ant." "Mmm, this is good."

"It was getting so late, I decided to go ahead and feed her," Abby said. "I hope you don't mind."

"Are you kidding? I appreciate it," Jack assured her. "But where's Millie?"

"She left," Kitty said.

Dumbfounded, he stared at her. "She *what?*"

"She said she had an appointment to get to, and when Ms. Walsh said she'd stay with me, Millie left," Kitty explained in a patient, adult-sounding tone that, under other circumstances, probably would have amused him.

Under these circumstances, however, he was anything but amused. He turned to Abby. "I'm sorry. I never intended for you to get roped into babysitting."

"She *likes* bein' with me," Kitty interrupted with a frown. "She *said* so."

He leaned down and kissed the top of her head. "Of course, she does, Kitten, but I'll bet Ms. Walsh had plans of her own for this evening."

Abby raised one shoulder in a negligent shrug. "Nothing that couldn't wait. We've had a productive afternoon."

She looked so damn cute standing there in a bright red T-shirt and a pair of baggy denim shorts, he wanted to kiss her head, too. But with Abby, he'd want to move on to her eyebrows, her cheekbones, her nose. And then her smiling lips.

He gazed into her eyes. Her cheeks turned an intense shade of pink, and he realized with another intuitive jolt that she was thinking similar thoughts. Oh, man, what was he supposed to do with that?

He forced his mind back to the conversation. "Really? What did you do?"

"She helped me do school stuff," Kitty said. "Math and reading."

"That's great," he said, his gaze still connected

with Abby's, an odd sort of communication flowing between them.

Feeling incredibly vulnerable, Abby blinked, turned away and stirred the soup. Her cheeks burned and the rest of her body tingled, and it didn't take a genius to figure out why. Holy smokes, he'd been looking at her with a hunger in his eyes that belonged in the bedroom, not the kitchen.

And she'd responded. She couldn't even try to pretend otherwise. This was exactly what she'd feared would happen when she saw him again.

Lord, he knew exactly what she'd been thinking. And feeling. And wishing. And he'd been thinking and feeling and wishing the same things.

She'd seen it all in those blue eyes that had dominated her thoughts since Saturday night. If she had one lick of sense, she'd be mortified, afraid...at the very least, extremely cautious. Instead, she felt excited. Fluttery. Alive.

Any thought of professional distance evaporated like the steam rising from the soup pot.

She heard his footsteps coming toward her, sensed his big body behind her, felt his breath ruffle her hair. He leaned closer, looking over her shoulder. Her heart rate zoomed and her temperature climbed a good five degrees.

"That's tortilla soup?" he asked.

"Right now, it's just tomato," she said, going for a light note and getting a breathless one, instead. "It'll become tortilla soup when I toss some chips on top."

"Interesting."

Glancing up, she saw he was looking at her, not the soup, and his whimsical smile drew her gaze to his mouth and held it there. His smile deepened. He raised one hand to the side of her head as if he wanted to touch her hair, hesitated, then lowered it to her shoulder and gave it an awkward pat. Beneath her T-shirt her skin heated where his fingers had made contact.

"I'll—" He cleared his throat and tried again. "I'll get washed and be right back."

When he left the room, Abby released a pent-up breath and hurried to flip over the sandwiches before they burned. She turned back to find Kitty carefully finishing another layer of celery sticks. The plate now held enough ants on a log for a family of six, but so what? Kitty would eat a bunch and the nutrition would do her good.

Abby wiped excess peanut butter off Kitty's hands, helped her carry the plate to the table, and hurriedly put the finishing touches on the simple meal. Whether or not he was there, being in Jack's home was too intimate for her comfort. She'd accomplished what she'd needed to do here, and now it was time for her to go home.

He returned to the kitchen, looked at the table and frowned at the two place settings. "You're not leaving, are you?"

Giving him a nervous smile, Abby slung her satchel over her shoulder and edged toward the doorway. "It's time for you to have dinner."

"Don't you want some?" Kitty asked.

"No, honey," Abby said with a smile. "This is your special time with your daddy. I don't want to intrude."

"When you cook, you can't intrude," Jack said.

He crossed the room, lifted the satchel's strap from

her shoulder and set it on the counter, then escorted her to the table, leaving her no graceful way to refuse. Bemused, she took a seat opposite Kitty and watched him go to work. He moved quickly and efficiently, setting another place, making another sandwich and dropping it into the skillet, then dividing the soup into three bowls.

The soup and sandwiches were delicious. Or perhaps it was having such pleasant company that made it seem so tasty. After the first few bites, Abby didn't care. She and Kitty and Jack were together, and they were having fun.

But even while she shared laughter and teasing glances with them, Abby was aware of a piercing sadness playing in the back of her mind for a woman she'd never met. From what she'd seen, Jack's wife had truly had it all—the love of a handsome, intelligent, wonderful man; a bright, adorable child and the promise of more children to come; a beautiful home in a lovely setting.

Gina had experienced so much more of family life than Abby herself ever would. But to think of everything Gina Granger had already missed and would miss in the future broke Abby's heart. She felt the same sadness for Kitty and Jack. Losing such an important person from their family circle was still devastating them.

And yet, there still was so much ahead for them.

Abby suspected she'd been drawn into their lives for a reason. The universe sometimes operated in bizarre ways, but if she could help them find a path to renewed happiness, she would be well satisfied with her efforts on their behalf. Then she could start her new life in Portland with no regrets.

In the meantime, maybe she ought to stop worrying so much about getting too involved. Why shouldn't she relax and enjoy whatever time she could spend with these two special people this summer? She wasn't taking anything away from Jack's wife, and as long as Abby remembered that this sense of family was only temporary, she wouldn't get hurt. Right? She could always hope.

All too soon the food disappeared. Jack sent Kitty upstairs to get ready for bed, and Abby found herself alone with him in the kitchen. He sat across the table, looking at her, a glint of devilry in his eyes and a wicked grin on his mouth.

Her pulse quickened. It was harder to breathe, as if he'd sucked most of the oxygen out of the room. She couldn't believe the wretched man was turning her on with his eyes and a stupid grin. But he was. She looked back at him, nerves screaming, and tried not to let Jack see her discomfort.

She held her own until he leaned closer, bracing one elbow on the table and resting his chin in his palm, as if making himself comfortable enough to carry on like this forever.

"What?" she said.

"What do you mean, what?" he asked.

"Stop staring at me like that."

"Oh, am I staring?"

"Yes, and I want you to stop it."

"But I really like looking at you." He gave her a soulful, puppy-dog look that made her want to laugh, kiss him and hit him, all at the same time. "What's wrong with that?"

"It's rude. And if that's all you're going to do, cut

it out.'' Jeez, she couldn't believe she'd actually said that. His staring must have fried her brain.

His grin deepened. His eyebrows arched in unmistakable challenge. ''What else do you want me to do, Abby?''

Oh, he thought he was so darn smart. And he *was* darn smart—but if he thought he was going to provoke her like this and walk away unscathed, he was about to learn otherwise. Slowly licking her upper lip, she leaned closer and lowered her voice.

''What do you *think* I want, Jack?''

His eyes widened. His nostrils flared. And then, as fast as a roadrunner, he was on her side of the table, grasping her upper arms and pulling her to her feet. His mouth came down on hers with no pretense of hesitation or gentleness—but she didn't want gentleness.

This time she wanted to feel his strength, his pleasure in kissing her, his raw desire for her. Once again, he gave her exactly what she wanted. Dear heaven, that other kiss *hadn't* been a fluke. With that last rational thought, she sank into the delicious madness of kissing him back.

There was heat and light and the heady excitement that had stayed in her consciousness since Saturday night. He pulled her against him and delved deeper into her mouth with his tongue. Her knees turned to the consistency of finger paint, forcing her to cling to his shoulders in order to stay upright.

He pulled her closer. Then, without releasing her mouth, he picked her up, sat down on her chair and settled her facing him on his lap. Supporting her back with his hands, he took the kiss even deeper. She slid her fingers into his hair, clasping the sides of his head with her palms, tasting him, stroking his tongue with her own and wanting more.

Always wanting more.

She should stop this now, but she didn't want to. In all honesty, she wanted this kiss to last forever. She felt so aroused, so fast, that she was dizzy with it; her body became a greedy, lustful thing she could barely control. It had been too long—far, far too long—since she'd known any sort of sexual satisfaction.

Her breasts felt heavy and ached with a need to be touched. Her hips rocked forward, straining to rub the ultrasensitive spot between her thighs against the hard ridge beneath the fly of his trousers. He made a low, groaning sound deep in his throat and lowered his hands to her bottom.

So excited she could barely breathe, she waited in an agony of anticipation. His fingertips tightened and lifted—

"Dad-dy!" Kitty hollered from upstairs. "I'm ready for my stor-ies!"

Abby and Jack both jerked as if they'd been doused with ice water. There was an impatient note in Kitty's voice suggesting this wasn't the first time she'd called. Fearing she might come downstairs to see what was keeping her daddy, Abby scrambled off Jack's lap.

Her knees were still mushy, but she turned away and wrapped her arms around herself, struggling to still an inner trembling born of frustration due to the untimely interruption. Or maybe it had been timely. It all depended on how she chose to look at it. Honestly, she knew better than to ditch her common sense when sexual attraction was involved.

Behind her, she heard Jack take a couple of deep, ragged-sounding breaths and walk to the doorway, calling, "I'll be right up, Kitten."

Abby turned around to face him and felt a thrill zing through her at the heat in his gaze, even while she instinctively stepped back, putting more space between them. Lord, she needed to get out of here. Now.

"Well, um…" Giving him what felt like a shaky smile, she walked to the counter holding her satchel. "I'll be going now so you can take care of Kitty."

He nodded with obvious reluctance. "All right, Abby. We'll talk later about what just happened."

"Oh, there's no need for that." She slung the strap over her shoulder and opened the back door. "Now that we've got that out of our systems, it won't be a problem."

Stunned by what she'd said, Jack watched Abby scoot through the door and close it behind her.

"Out of our systems?" he muttered, laughing and shaking his head in amazement. "In your dreams, babe."

Chapter Nine

"Aren't you going to be late for work?" Millie asked on the following Monday morning, when she saw Jack sitting at the kitchen table. She tossed her purse onto the counter and reached for the coffeepot in one smooth motion.

"I'm going in late today." Jack ran nervous fingers through his hair. "I wanted to talk to you before we left. Kitty's had a lousy weekend. The nightmares have come back, she wet the bed twice and she had a full-blown, screaming tantrum on Saturday."

"Oh, the poor little thing." Millie filled her own cup and gave Jack a refill before sitting opposite him. "That doesn't even sound like her."

"She did this before when she had therapy. Dr. Johnson assures me it just means she's getting closer to a breakthrough. With any luck, it won't last too long. I'll be taking her to see Dr. Johnson this morning, but I don't know what kind of shape she'll be in when we come home.''

Millie pursed her lips. ''Then, don't you think you should take the whole day off and stay with her, dear?''

''I would if I could, but I have to be in court this afternoon.'' She opened her mouth, and he held up one hand to cut her off. ''This isn't a case I can delegate on such short notice. The defendant has a good lawyer. He tried to kill his wife, and I wouldn't put it past him to try it again if he gets off.''

Millie's forehead wrinkled up with worry lines. ''I understand, but I'm a better housekeeper than I am a baby-sitter. If Kitty gets upset, you know it won't be me she wants.''

''It won't be me, either,'' Jack said, feeling completely out of his depth. ''She'll want Abby. I already asked Abby if she'd be willing to come over later if Kitty needs her. Thank God, she said yes.''

''I'll call her.'' Millie sipped from her coffee mug. After a moment, she winked at him. ''You know, that pretty little teacher's awfully good for Kitty. She'd make a fine mother for your little girl.''

''I agree.'' Jack smiled at Millie's surprised expression. ''I'm way ahead of you on this one.''

''Are you, now?'' Millie grinned and leaned closer, lowering her voice. ''Want to tell me what's been going on?''

''Let's just say I'm working on it.''

''Good. Well, let me know if you need any help, dear. I can always put in a good word for you. Woman to woman.''

''Thanks, but I can manage,'' he said dryly.

''Whatever you say.'' She leaned back against the

cabinets and crossed her arms over her chest. "But maybe you shouldn't have gotten so mad at me when I left early last Monday. It gave you a chance to spend time with Abby, didn't it?"

Appalled at the thought Millie might interfere in his courtship plans, even with the best of intentions, Jack shook his head and held up both hands. "No. Please, stay out of this. Abby still thinks we're just going to be friends. She's not ready for anything else, so please don't say a word to her."

"Don't be silly, dear. I won't mess up anything for you."

Hardly reassured, he shook his head again, but before he could say anything, Kitty straggled into the kitchen, her face pale, dark circles under her eyes and her hair already coming out of the ponytail holder he'd put in not ten minutes ago.

"Good morning, Kitty," Millie said.

Kitty gave her a halfhearted smile, then turned to Jack. "I'm ready now, Daddy."

"Okay, Kitten." Taking her hand, Jack led her to the kitchen door.

Millie smiled and wiggled her fingers in what he supposed was meant to be a friendly little wave. Jack paused long enough to send her one last warning frown, then took Kitty outside to the car. He could have sworn he heard his housekeeper laughing quietly, but he didn't have time to deal with her now. He had more important things to handle first.

The phone rang, shattering Abby's deep concentration on her dissertation. She picked up the cordless phone, but before she could even say hello, she heard

Millie Patten talking in a loud, panicked voice on the other end of the line.

"Oh, thank goodness, you're home." Millie sounded as if she might be hyperventilating. "I need your help. It's Kitty."

"What happened?" Abby punched Save on the computer, then carried the phone as she raced into her bedroom for her sandals.

"She came home from that appointment with Dr. Johnson, and seemed okay for a while. But when I asked her to come outside and help me water the flowers, she pitched a real fit and locked herself in the bathroom. That was thirty minutes ago, and I can't get her to come out to save my life. Can you come over here?"

"I'm on my way. Ten minutes, max."

Grabbing her purse and car keys, Abby tossed the phone on the kitchen counter and rushed out the door. After a frantic drive to Jack's place, she ran into the house without knocking, following the sound of Millie's voice up the stairs. The housekeeper was on her knees in front of the bathroom door.

"Kitty, honey, you've got to come out—"

Millie sounded so exasperated, Abby thought that if she were Kitty's age, she wouldn't come out of the bathroom, either.

"You're scaring me, sweetheart."

Abby patted Millie's shoulder. The older woman flinched, then twisted around, her eyes wide with alarm.

"Sorry," Abby murmured. "I didn't mean to startle you."

"That's all right." Millie uttered a shaky laugh. "I'm just glad you're here."

Abby tilted her head toward the bathroom door. "Is there anything in there she can hurt herself with? Medicine? Cleaners?"

"No, Jack's always been real careful to keep stuff like that locked up."

"Good. We can afford to wait her out." Abby smiled. "Why don't you go take a break? I'll see what I can do with Kitty."

"Good luck." Millie held out a hand. Her knees made crackling sounds when Abby helped her to her feet. "I'll try to get Jack on the phone again."

"Fine." Abby waited until the housekeeper reached the first floor, then sat on the hall carpet Indian-style and called to Kitty. "Hey, Miss Kitty. What's going on?"

"M-M-Ms. Walsh?"

Abby winced at the pain in Kitty's teary little voice, but she kept her own voice calm and matter-of-fact. "It's me, all right. Why don't you come out and say hello?"

"Don't want to."

"Okay. What are you doing in there?"

"N-n-nuthin'."

"Isn't that kind of boring?" Abby asked.

"A little."

"Want me to slide a book under the door? You could read it to me."

"Don't f-feel like r-reading."

"What *do* you feel like doing, sweetie?"

"Nuthin'."

"Oh, that's too bad," Abby said, trying to sound terribly disappointed. "I was hoping you'd...well, never mind."

There was a long silence. Just when Abby was

about to give up and try another approach, Kitty asked, "What were you hoping?"

"It's nothing important," Abby said. "I just thought maybe you'd like to come over to my apartment and go swimming with me this afternoon."

"I don't have a swimming suit. Mine's too small."

"That's not a problem," Abby assured her. "We'll just stop at a store and buy one. That is, if you'd like to go."

"I don't know how to swim." Kitty let out a big sigh that ended on a sob. "I took lessons before, but I don't remember what I'm s'posed to do."

"That's okay, sweetie. I can teach you."

"I prob'ly can't do it, anyway. I'm not good at anything."

She started to cry in earnest. It was the loneliest sound Abby had ever heard. She didn't know how long she could stand listening to the child's heart breaking before she ripped down that door with her bare hands.

"You just need to practice, Kitty— You sound like you need a big hug. Please, unlock the door and let me give you one."

"You'll b-be m-mad at m-me. So will M-M-Millie. And my d-daddy will, t-too."

"No, honey. We know you've been having a hard time. Nobody will be mad at you."

"What if I wet my pants?"

"It's all right. We'll just clean you up, and nobody else has to know about it."

"You promise?"

"I promise. You'd be amazed at how many kids have accidents like that at school. Let me in now. I only want to help you."

Kitty was so quiet, Abby shifted onto her knees and pressed her ear against the door, straining to hear something that would give her an idea what the little girl was doing. An eternity later there was soft *click* and the door slowly inched open. Abby held her breath until Kitty's swollen, tear-streaked face appeared in the narrow gap between the door and its casing.

Crawling forward, Abby gently pushed with one hand, widening the opening until she could enter the room. She'd barely made it inside before Kitty hurled herself into her arms. Once again, Abby held the weeping child close, rocking her back and forth, while Kitty's hot tears soaked the front of her blouse.

"Shh, baby," Abby murmured. "It's all right now. Everything's going to be all right."

Kitty cried so hard, for so long, Abby feared they would have to ask a doctor to come and sedate her. At long last, however, the little girl quieted, leaning against Abby in an exhausted stupor. Abby wet a washcloth and bathed Kitty, then helped her into clean panties and a T-shirt and tucked her in bed for a nap.

Already nodding off, Kitty murmured, "Can we still go swimming?"

"You bet we can," Abby said, gently squeezing her little hand. "Just rest now, honey. That's all you need to do."

"'Kay. Love you, Ms. Walsh."

Tears burned Abby's eyes, but she held them back long enough to whisper, "I love you, too, Kitty."

Then she fled from the room, quietly shutting the door and hurrying downstairs to the kitchen. The instant she saw Millie's red eyes and the wad of soggy tissues in her hand, Abby lost it. Tears flooded her eyes and poured down her face. "Oh, Millie, we've got to help her."

Handing Abby a box of tissues, Millie dabbed at her own cheeks. "I know, but when the poor little tyke gets like that, I just don't know what to do for her."

The back door opened. Jack rushed inside, took one look at them and stopped dead in his tracks, his face turning pale. "What happened? Where's Kitty?"

"She's taking a nap," Abby said with a sniffle. "She's okay now."

"Then, why are you two crying?" he asked.

"Because she's so sad, it's breaking our hearts," Millie said. "The poor little dear is just falling apart."

Jack's shoulders sagged as if the weight of the planet had just descended on them. He set his briefcase on the floor and wiped one hand down over his face. "I talked with Dr. Johnson for a long time this morning. She gave me some suggestions, but I don't know if they'll work."

Abby crossed the room and took his hand between both of hers. "You can't afford to get discouraged now, Jack. Why don't we all have something cold to drink and talk about it?"

"That's your cure for everything, isn't it. Talking."

"It's the only thing I know of that usually works."

"Right." He gave her a tired smile. "Let me check on Kitty and get out of this suit. Then I'll be all yours."

Abby froze. Feet rooted to the floor, she watched him walk out of the kitchen, her heart thumping hard against her rib cage in response to his last four words.

He hadn't meant that the way it had sounded. Of course, he hadn't. But, sweet heaven, she wished he *had* meant it that way.

Oh, jeez, she was in big trouble here. It wasn't bad enough that she'd already fallen in love with Kitty? Now she had to have tender feelings for Jack, too? Did she even have a choice anymore?

Jack looked in on Kitty, a lump the size of a baseball lodging in his throat while he studied her puffy little face. Even in sleep, her forehead was creased with anxiety, and she was sucking her thumb as vigorously as she had at two.

Oh God, she was his responsibility, but what if he really couldn't help her? Sheer terror for her well-being washed over him, misting his skin with a cold sweat and sending his heart rate into overdrive. Then Abby's words came back to him.

"You can't afford to get discouraged now, Jack."

Abby was right. Just as she'd been right about so many other things. Wondering how she'd gotten so wise at such a young age, he leaned down, gently kissed Kitty's forehead and silently left the room.

When he arrived back downstairs wearing an old pair of jeans and a T-shirt, Abby and Millie were sitting on opposite sides of the kitchen table, each with a tall glass of iced tea. A third glass marked his place at the end of the table. He sat in front of it and took a long drink.

"What did Dr. Johnson say?" Millie asked.

Jack thought back to the morning's appointment, pulling up the pertinent information. "She thinks Kitty's making progress," he said. "The therapy's still pretty tough because Kitty's resisting something, but only Kitty knows what it is. Once we can figure that part out, the worst will be over.''

Millie heaved a tired sigh. ''How long will that take?''

''There's no way to tell,'' Abby said. ''Did Erin say anything about medication?''

Jack grimaced. ''Yeah, but I really don't like that idea, and I had the impression she didn't, either.''

''It may be necessary,'' Abby told him.

''I know. But first, I want to try her other suggestion.''

''What was that?'' Millie asked.

''She wants Kitty to be out in the sunshine more and get some good, hard exercise. Supposedly, that'll make her feel better.''

''It will,'' Abby agreed. ''It'll boost her endorphin levels just like an antidepressant, but she won't have to take any drugs.''

Millie went to the refrigerator and brought the pitcher of tea back to the table. ''Mercy, it won't be easy to get Kitty to cooperate. I was trying to take her outside with me when she had that…tantrum. I'm afraid I'm just too old to handle all of this.''

''I understand,'' Jack said. ''To be honest, I don't know what I'm going to do yet. I can't afford to quit working, but I know I've got to do something.''

''I could pick her up at noon every day and get her to exercise with me,'' Abby suggested. ''She could even stay with me until you get off work.''

''What about your dissertation?'' Jack asked. ''Don't you need that time for writing?''

''I do most of it in the morning. And if I really need to, I can figure out a way to get some more done while Kitty's with me.''

"That'd work fine," Millie said with a smile. "Could I still call you in an emergency?"

"Anytime," Abby assured her, then looked at Jack. "Is that all right with you?"

Her easy generosity had brought the baseball back to his throat. Uncertain if he could actually speak, he nodded, then took another long drink of tea. "That'd be great, if you'll promise to let me know when it starts feeling like an imposition."

"Now that we've got that settled and you're home early, I think I'll head out." Millie pushed back her chair and stood again. "See you tomorrow."

"'Bye, Millie," Abby said, keeping her eyes on Jack.

"How can I ever thank you enough?" he asked, his voice barely louder than a whisper.

"Don't try. I want to help her, too."

She reached across the table and found his hand. He turned his palm up and laced his fingers through hers.

"You really love Kitty, don't you."

Nodding slowly, she gave him a rueful smile. "Who wouldn't?"

"Are you kidding?" He laughed. "Kitty's not exactly Little Miss Sunshine right now."

Abby's eyes darkened with an emotion he couldn't readily identify, but there was no mistaking the compassion in her voice. "She's in pain, Jack. That doesn't make her any less lovable."

"I agree, but there are plenty of people who wouldn't feel that way. If I haven't mentioned it before now, I'm really glad you're here. You wouldn't believe what a huge relief it is not to have to go through all of this alone." He paused long enough to swallow, then squeezed Abby's hand. "When Gina died, I kept thinking it should've been me, because she knew so much more about raising children than I did."

"What happened to her?"

"The doctor called it a hypertrophic cardiomyopathy, which is a fancy way of saying she had an inherited heart defect. She never mentioned having any symptoms, but sometimes there aren't any. One day when she went to her aerobics class, she just suddenly went into heart failure and died."

"Did they do CPR on her?"

"They tried, but she was gone by the time the paramedics arrived. It was one of those freak things you hear about when a high school or college athlete keels over and dies with the team doctor standing right there."

"That's so sad, Jack."

He shrugged because he knew his eyes would fill with tears if he tried to answer that, and he wouldn't cry in front of Abby. "We were lucky it didn't happen while she was driving with Kitty in the car."

"Where was Kitty?"

"At her play group. She went there whenever Gina needed a break." He shut his eyes and pinched the bridge of his nose with his thumb and forefinger. "The hardest thing I've ever had to do was tell her that Mommy wasn't going to come back."

"Have you talked about this with anyone?" Abby asked softly.

"I was afraid to at first," he admitted.

"Why?"

He didn't know how anyone could put such empathy into one word, but he answered the question as honestly as he would have done with Gina. "I thought I might fall apart, and I couldn't risk it because Kitty really needed me."

"I'm sure she did. But what about later?"

"Gina had been my best friend since high school. There wasn't anyone else I wanted to talk to." He squeezed her hand again. "Until now. You're the world's best listener."

"Thanks." She wrapped her other hand around the back of his. "Everybody needs to be heard sometimes."

"Oh, yeah? Who do you talk to?"

"Erin got me through my divorce." Abby gave him a sad smile. "She sees way too much for comfort sometimes, but she gives wonderful advice."

He hesitated for a moment before asking, "Could you ever talk to me?"

"About what?"

"I don't know. What happened to your marriage, maybe. Whatever you need to talk about."

She frowned in confusion. "What are you really asking?"

"I want to be your friend, but I'm feeling a little exposed here. You know everything about me, but I don't know anything about you."

"Maybe someday."

"Only maybe?"

"Probably," she conceded. "Right now, you need to save your energy for Kitty. She's going to be fine, you know. You're doing all the right things for her."

"How do you *do* that?" he asked.

"Do what?"

"You make me feel okay about myself when I don't deserve to," he said. "You do the same thing

for Kitty and you don't even think about it. You're
incredibly accepting of other people's faults.''

She laughed. ''It's not as if I don't have any of my
own, Jack. You saw them the first time we met.''

''I don't see them at all, now.'' Bracing his elbow
on the corner of the table, he leaned closer. ''I can't
even remember what they were.''

She wrinkled her nose at him and tossed her head,
flipping her ponytail behind her shoulder. ''If you're
waiting for me to remind you, you're going to have
a very long wait.''

He'd bet his law degree she didn't have a clue how
adorable she looked at that moment. Her eyes glinted
with amusement and mischief. Her lips wore a pouty
little smile that practically begged to be kissed.

''I wouldn't believe you, anyway.'' He reached
out, curved his fingers around the back of her head
and tipped her chin up with his thumb. Then he lowered his head and kissed her with all the tenderness
he could muster. He started with her lips and slowly
nibbled his way across her cheekbones, her eyelids,
her eyebrows and the tip of her nose.

Though he wanted her with an ache that went all
the way through him, he'd promised himself he
wouldn't rush her. She'd opened her heart wide for
his daughter, and he couldn't—no—*wouldn't*—push
her for anything more than she was already giving
him. With this kiss, he wanted to show her how much
he valued her as a friend and a confidante.

But her skin was incredibly soft and smooth under
his lips, her ponytail felt cool and silky against the
back of his hand and she smelled like sunshine and
wildflowers. He returned to her sweet mouth. She

parted her lips, inviting him to deepen the kiss—and at the first taste of her, he was lost.

She came out of her chair and around to his end of the table, crossing her wrists at the back of his neck. Her tongue darted into his mouth, skating along the edges of his teeth, teasing the tip of his tongue with shy touches, then stroking the roof of his mouth. He tasted a hint of the lemon from her tea and smiled at the incongruous combination of sourness and the sweetest kisses in the world.

"What are you smiling at?" she asked in a sultry, amused voice that tickled his nerve endings like a feather.

"You." He spread his knees apart and pulled her between them. "For such a little thing, you're a great kisser."

"Is that supposed to be a compliment?"

"Oh, yeah. I've always felt big and awkward around people like you."

"People like me? What's that supposed to mean?"

"Short people."

"I'm not short."

He would have laughed, but she'd looked so serious when she said that, he wasn't sure if she was putting him on. "You don't think so?"

"Of course not. I'm as tall as I need to be. You, on the other hand, are too tall. You're the one who's got a problem."

In spite of his efforts to suppress it, laughter bubbled out of him. "I'm a man, Abby."

"Believe me, I'm aware of that." She grinned, then rubbed the tip of her nose against his. "So what?"

"Men are supposed to be tall, strong and hairy." He ran his hands up her sides, straying close to her breasts with his thumbs, but not actually touching them. He loved the way her breathing hitched every time he moved his hands upward, the way she sighed when he reversed direction. "Women are supposed to be curvy, soft and smaller. You, however, are *short.*"

She gave him a ferocious frown that made him laugh again. "I'll show you *short,* buster."

Plunging her hands into his hair, she rubbed his scalp with her fingertips until he wanted to purr like a tiger. At the same time, she stroked her thumbs over the curves of his ears in the exact same motion he was using on her sides, and his own breathing caught in response. He splayed one hand across her back, wrapped her ponytail around his other hand and took her mouth in a deep, wet kiss that short-circuited his thought processes and left him feeling greedy and possessive.

Her knees buckled, and the tips of her breasts brushed against his chest. He pulled her sideways onto his lap. Heat surged through him like a high fever; his heartbeat pounded in his ears. She held on to the back of his head as if it might kill her if he stopped kissing her. As if he could.

He slid his right hand up her side and cupped her breast—she froze. He pulled back immediately, but her eyelids flew open and she stared blankly at him for a moment before the confusion cleared from her eyes and she struggled to sit upright. Biting back a curse, he helped her, sucking in a harsh breath in an attempt to settle himself down.

"I—I'm...I'm sorry," she stammered, looking over his shoulder, at the ceiling, anywhere but at his face. "I didn't mean to get so carried away."

Hell. The last thing he wanted was for her to feel

ashamed of her own natural responses. Curving his fingers around her cheek, he coaxed her into meeting his gaze.

"You weren't the only one who got carried away." His voice sounded rougher than he would have liked, but his body was still so strongly protesting the idea of stopping short of satisfaction, he was lucky not to be snarling at her. "And you know what, Abby?"

A relieved smile tugged at the corners of her mouth. Still, as if she sensed the struggle taking place inside him, she kept her own voice at a whisper.

"What?"

"I don't think either one of us has got this out of our system."

Chapter Ten

Jack's words haunted Abby during the next five weeks. As the days passed, however, it felt perfectly natural to spend more and more time with him and Kitty. Being with them, though, made her feel like a penniless kid with her nose pressed against the toy store window. Everything she'd ever wanted was right there in front of her, but still completely out of her reach.

Though she avoided touching Jack as much as possible, her attraction to him grew at an alarming rate. She couldn't even blame it on him, either. The rat. Oh, he flirted with her sometimes, and stole an occasional kiss, but he didn't actively try to seduce her.

She could hardly complain about that; the man was only doing what he'd said he would—keeping their relationship on a casual basis. She admired him for keeping his promise. Even more, she appreciated having time to know him better without a lot of pressure to have sex.

Unfortunately, whenever he was around or if she simply thought about him, she felt a sexual thrill she couldn't deny or ignore. She'd caught enough heated glances and heard enough strangled sighs to suspect he was suffering as much frustration as she was. Lord, she hoped so. She'd never been this attracted to anyone. Ever.

But she couldn't give in to it. There was no hope of a future for them. End of story.

Right.

She wished it were that simple.

Half the time, she could barely remember the reasons she wasn't supposed to get involved with him. *In a few short weeks she would be gone. She had big dreams and goals to pursue. She was never going to have another serious relationship with a man.* It shouldn't be so hard to keep them in mind.

The only thing that helped her maintain her sense of balance was developing a comfortable routine. She zealously guarded her mornings for work on her dissertation. But her day really began when she shut down her computer at 11:45 to go to pick up Kitty.

Some days were better than others, of course. After an appointment with Erin, Kitty tended to be tearful and reluctant to do anything. Abby would have to tease and bribe and even nag the poor kid into leaving the house, but she always won. After one of Millie's nutritious lunches, Abby and Kitty took off for an afternoon of activity that dramatically improved the child's appetite and sleeping patterns. Gradually, Kitty started to feel better.

They hiked in the woods and waded in creeks, went

to parks and floated down the Little Spokane River on big, black inner tubes. They took Rollerblading lessons at a nearby rink, then practiced their new skills on the school's empty parking lot. When they were hot and tired, they drove to Abby's apartment and splashed around in the pool.

Before long, Kitty demanded swimming lessons, which Abby happily supplied. A snack and a tutoring session followed pool time, lasting until Jack arrived. The three of them usually ate dinner together. Afterward, they often went out for a movie, played miniature golf or took another swim or rented a video to watch together.

If Kitty should happen to fall asleep, which she often did, Abby and Jack talked for hours about anything and everything, getting acquainted and learning to feel comfortable with each other.

On the Fourth of July, they took a picnic down to Riverfront Park and sat on a blanket across the river from the Opera House, surrounded by thousands of other people who'd come to enjoy the symphony concert and watch the fireworks. Snuggling into Abby's arms, Kitty *ooh*ed and *aah*ed over each explosion of color, her eyes glowing with wonder at the spectacle.

Aching inside for all the moments like this she'd missed by not having a child of her own, Abby blinked back tears and cuddled Kitty closer, knowing she was making memories to cherish for a lifetime.

Jack sauntered into her apartment one night a week later, carrying a deli chicken salad for their dinner. He set it on the kitchen counter and scooped Kitty into his arms for a hug. Grinning wickedly, he slapped a couple of entry forms for the annual Cherry

Pickers' Trot on the table. "I hereby challenge you to a race, Ms. Walsh."

"I'm already registered," she said, then shot him a worried frown. "Are you sure you're up to this?"

He laughed off her concern. "Don't worry about me."

"That's a tough course," she warned. "It's four miles. The last two are straight uphill and the temperature's usually in the nineties. If you're not in shape—"

"I can run, woman." He thumped his chest with one hand. "I'll have you know I was on the cross-country team in high school."

"And how long ago was that? Fifteen years? Sixteen?"

"What's the matter, Walsh?" He stepped closer, leering as he loomed over her. "Afraid I'll win?"

"I don't think so." She laughed, then poked her index finger at his sternum. "I just hope you don't pout when you lose."

"I don't intend to lose." He leaned down and kissed the tip of her nose. "I've been training on my lunch hour."

"For how long?"

"None of your business."

"Dad-dy," Kitty said, looking from one of them to the other in wide-eyed fascination, "you kissed Ms. Walsh!"

"Who me?" He shared an amused glance with Abby. "No way."

Kitty shrieked with laughter. "You did so."

He continued to play the outraged innocent. "I wouldn't do a thing like that. I don't even *like* girls."

He swooped down and kissed the tip of Kitty's little nose. "Except for you."

"But you kissed Ms. Walsh," Kitty insisted. "I saw you. And you're supposed to tell the truth."

"You tell him, Kitty," Abby said.

The bantering among them continued right up until the night of the race. Millie offered to come along and watch Kitty, while Jack and Abby ran the course. They all piled into Abby's Bronco for the drive out to Green Bluff, a tiny community north of Spokane known for its apple and cherry orchards.

Wandering through the crowd, they watched the pit-spitting contest and bought Kitty and Millie barbecued burgers for supper. Jack found them a place to sit where they could eat and listen to the country-and-western band, then accompanied Abby to stand in line for their T-shirts.

Aware that Jack was receiving plenty of female attention, Abby snuck a glance at him and felt her face heat and her mouth go dry. Uh-oh, she'd been so wrapped up in helping Kitty get ready and making sure they all had everything they needed, she hadn't noticed what Jack was wearing. Or wasn't wearing. He always looked wonderful to her, but his business suits covered up some of his more spectacular attributes—tanned, muscular arms and shoulders, a lean torso, a tight, flat belly and powerful legs that stretched on forever, to name a few.

The first time she'd seen him in swimming trunks she'd had to dive under the water to hide her lustful reaction. The skimpy blue running shorts and the tank top he had on now were having a similar effect. On closer inspection of his thighs and his butt, she decided maybe he really had been training on his lunch hour.

She could only hope everyone would blame her red face on the heat rather than the erotic images playing through her mind.

"Jack? Jack Granger? Is that really you?" a cultured female voice called from the next line over. "Look, Kent, it's Jack."

Jack turned, and Abby automatically turned with him in time to see an attractive couple hurrying toward them. Half a head shorter than Jack and about the same age, the man had black hair, brown eyes and the beginnings of a paunch. The woman was a redhead with blue eyes, an improbably perfect figure and flashy jewelry. They both wore shorts outfits with designer labels and state-of-the-art walking shoes.

The man shook Jack's hand. The woman leaned very close, brushing her breasts against Jack's chest while she went up on her tiptoes to kiss his cheek. Then they both turned to her, their eyes sharp with curiosity.

"Abby, this is Kent and Nadine Murphy," Jack said. "Kent and I started out at the prosecutor's office together. Kent, Nadine, this is Abby Walsh."

"I didn't realize Jack was dating anyone," Nadine said, subtly pulling Abby aside while her husband talked to Jack. "How long have you known each other?"

Seeing she was about to be grilled by an expert, Abby decided to be honest, but share as little information as possible. "I've known him about a year."

Nadine's eyes widened, then crinkled at the corners in what was probably supposed to have been a smile, but looked more like a grimace. "Oh, then, you must've met dear little Kathleen by now."

"Yes, she's a sweetie."

Nadine waited, as if she expected Abby to say more. After a moment's silence, Nadine continued. "How are they getting along without Gina?"

"They seem to be doing fine." Okay, so that was a fib, but Abby couldn't imagine Jack would want her to discuss Kitty's problems with this…woman.

"It was absolutely the saddest thing in the world." Nadine briefly closed her eyes, as if memories of Gina Granger caused her considerable pain. "Aside from the personal devastation, it's had a terrible effect on Jack's career."

Abby uttered a noncommittal "Mmm."

Nadine needed no further encouragement. "She was the perfect lawyer's wife, if you know what I mean."

"I'm afraid I don't."

"Well, she kept a lovely home, entertained the right people and served on the best charity committees." Nadine's gaze drifted down over Abby, and her upper lip curled into a faint sneer. "Gina was beautiful and had the most elegant fashion sense you can imagine. If she'd lived to manage Jack's social obligations and maintain his contacts, he'd be a congressman or a judge in five years. That was her goal."

Abby wondered if that had been *Jack's* goal, too. Nadine obviously intended to wound with her observations, and Abby had a strong urge to claw the woman's eyes out. The strength of her desire for violence surprised her, until she realized Nadine had accomplished what she'd set out to do. Abby felt threatened and jealous—fiercely jealous of Gina

Granger, the perfect lawyer's wife. Fertility issues aside, Abby knew she could never measure up to Jack's wife.

The whole thing was irrational and ridiculous. Abby had her own talents and strengths, and she wasn't in a competition with anyone for Jack's affections. That was so high school. Or maybe even junior high.

It just went to show that her feelings for Jack were becoming too personal, too important, too close to love for her own good. Time to reassess this relationship. And she would, just as soon as this race was over and she had some time alone. Perhaps she should consider leaving for Portland sooner than she'd planned. She really didn't want to, but it might be wiser.

Jack breathed a quiet sigh of relief when the Murphys went back to their own T-shirt line. He'd never really liked either of them, and neither had Gina, but there was no point in making enemies, particularly in his business. He glanced down at Abby, noting her worried expression. What had Nadine said to upset her? He was about to ask Abby about it, when she poked him in the ribs.

She nodded toward the table in front of him. "Your turn to get a shirt."

They collected their shirts, dropped them off with Millie and went for a warm-up jog. He liked running with Abby, liked the smooth way she ran, liked that she didn't let her hair or makeup get in the way of having fun.

When they reached the starting line, he grinned at her. "Don't hold back, Abby. If I can't keep up, it's my problem, not yours."

"What's this?" she demanded with a laugh. "An admission that you might not beat me?"

"I just want you to enjoy the race. Whatever happens, I promise not to whine."

"I can't tell you what a relief that is," she said dryly.

The starting gun sounded and the crowd surged forward. At first Jack's size gave him a decided advantage, as people tended to get out of his way. He couldn't see Abby anywhere. Once he broke out of the pack, she appeared at his side, and he realized she'd been behind him all along, letting him blaze a path.

She shot him a grin, then adjusted her pace to match his. Though she had to take two steps to every one of his, she stayed right with him. He'd forgotten how good it felt to work his body like this.

There was something incredibly sexy about moving in such perfect rhythm with each other. It was too hot even to think about talking, but they exchanged frequent smiles. They zipped through the first mile and the second. Then the road curved to the right and they were chugging up one hill after another, each one steeper than the last.

By the end of the third mile, his thigh and calf muscles burned along with his lungs, and sweat literally poured off him, but he kept going and so did Abby. His admiration for her strength and tenacity grew with every step. They crossed the finish line together, chests heaving as they gradually slowed to a walk.

"Not bad, Granger," she said, holding up her hand for a high-five.

"Thanks." He gently slapped her palm, then gave

her a one-armed hug. She slid her arm around his
waist and hugged him back for a second before she
pulled away, joking about being too sweaty to touch.
He immediately felt the loss. A vision of the two of
them sharing a lusty shower popped into his mind,
and he nearly tripped over his own feet.

She shot him an odd look, but Kitty and Millie
arrived to greet them, killing any chance of a private
moment.

The vision stayed with him during the ride home
and long after Abby had left for her apartment, leading him to an important conclusion. He'd been patient
forever, but he was more than ready to move their
relationship to a deeper level. He thought Abby was,
too, but he doubted she'd bring up the subject. The
summer was more than half over. If he wanted her to
change her mind about leaving, it was time to start
giving her reasons to stay.

Back at her apartment, Abby showered, pulled on
a clean pair of running shorts and a red tank top, and
piled her still-damp hair on top of her head, securing
it with a plastic clip. After raiding the refrigerator for
a salad and some iced tea, she sat at the kitchen table,
but found she didn't have an appetite. She was so
used to having Jack and Kitty here—the room was
too quiet, and it felt strange to eat alone.

She'd made the excuse that she needed the evening
to work on her dissertation, but she really just needed
time to think. About Jack. About Kitty. About how
she really felt about them as opposed to how she kept
telling herself she was *supposed* to feel. As if emotions were tangible things like little bottles of spices
that a person could keep neat and tidy on a shelf.

She got up, opened the sliding glass door and walked out onto the small balcony. Resting her forearms on the railing, she looked out over the street. What was she going to do about Jack and Kitty?

Truth was, she'd already done the unthinkable. She'd fallen in love with both of them. Without any conscious planning, the three of them had come together and formed a family of sorts. Abby tried to tell herself that it was only a temporary family, something to help Kitty get through her therapy. Once Kitty was all right, they would go their separate ways with no harm done and no sad feelings.

No, that was impossible. Kitty would be devastated when she left, and Abby knew it.

And Jack? Would he be devastated when she was gone?

If they felt even half of what Abby suspected *she* was going to feel, they would be inconsolable. Oh, yes, she was already in so deep, losing Jack and Kitty would be like losing two of her limbs.

When she looked at them, she didn't see just a handsome man and an adorable child. She saw two people who occupied a vitally important piece of her life—the piece that contained the laughter, joy and companionship that had made these long summer days the happiest she'd ever known. How she wished they never had to end.

Her life would go on without the small daily intimacies she now shared with Jack and Kitty. But it would never be the same. Part of her would always want them, miss them, belong to them.

Should she run away now and protect her tender heart from as much pain as she possibly could? No,

Kitty still needed her too much for her even to think about leaving. Jack did, too.

There was another possibility. She could open herself to them even more and relish every second she could share with them for the short time she'd allotted. No matter what she did now, it was going to hurt when she left. A chance like this might never come her way again.

Why not allow herself to feel like a real mother for a little while? Why not allow herself to enjoy being with a man she admired and respected? Why not get really honest and admit she wanted his body to a point approaching obsession?

Even during her marriage she'd never been this focused on sex. She'd never in her life lain awake for hours, imagining what it would be like to make love with a particular person, wishing she had the nerve to tell him. She'd certainly never had vivid, sexually inventive dreams about the same person night after night.

A couple of kisses from Jack had changed all that. Running with him tonight was only going to make it worse. Every time she closed her eyes now, she saw him gliding along beside her, strong arms and legs pumping, sweat glistening on his skin, his teeth flashing white against his tanned face.

He was the ultimate picture of a strong, healthy, handsome man who was in control of his body and knew how to feel pleasure. And how to give it. If that wasn't sexy, she didn't want to know what was.

She thought about him all the time with a craving that made her sympathize with anyone trying to beat an addiction. It was embarrassing to feel so preoccupied with carnal thoughts of a man she couldn't have. But *why* couldn't she have him?

He still wanted her; he'd made no secret of that. She'd been honest with him about her plans, so he wouldn't be expecting anything serious to develop. And it would only be for a few weeks. As long as she knew it was going to end, even *when* it was going to end, she could survive the inevitable parting.

Couldn't she?

Her doorbell rang. Though she couldn't have said why, she suspected it might be Jack. Heart soaring, she hurried to find out. After a glance in the peephole confirmed her suspicion, she swung the door open wide.

One hand behind his back, he stood there, wearing his favorite jeans and a crisply ironed, short-sleeved blue shirt, and looking at her as if he'd been starving for her. For weeks. Maybe months. The corners of his mouth turned up in a slow, heated smile that set off a curling sensation at the core of her body.

"Hi," he said.

"Hi." She drank in the sight of him, committing the smallest details of his appearance to memory. The small, pale scar above the crook in his right eyebrow. The first silver strands at his temples. The tiny dot of red on his chin where he'd nicked himself shaving. Recently. He ordinarily didn't shave at night....

"Mind if I come in?" His voice was low and just husky enough to make the fine hairs on the back of her neck prickle.

Wordlessly stepping out of his way, she watched him cross the threshold, knowing that by inviting him in, she was crossing an important threshold of her own. He brought his hand out from behind his back, offering her a large pink peony blossom, opened to its peak of perfection. She'd seen this very blossom growing on a bush in front of her apartment complex that afternoon and couldn't help laughing when she realized he'd stolen it for her.

"Thanks." She held it to her nose, inhaling the sweet fragrance before adding, "But you really shouldn't have."

"You make me want to do a lot of things I probably shouldn't."

"Where's Kitty?" she asked.

"At home. I'm on call this week, so Millie's staying over." He set a beeper and a cell phone on top of a bookcase and turned back to her. "I told her I was going out. And that I'd be late getting home."

Sinning shouldn't be this easy, Abby thought, fighting an urge to burst into hysterical laughter. "I see."

"Do you?" He stepped closer and tucked an index finger under her chin, raising it until she met his gaze head-on. "Do you have any idea how much I want you?"

"I think so."

"Does that mean you want me, too?"

She tried to speak, but her throat wouldn't cooperate. Looking at him with her heart in her eyes, she nodded.

"Oh, thank God."

He took the flower from her and set it beside his beeper, then wrapped his arms around her and held her close. She snuggled against him, sliding her arms around his torso and brushing her cheek over his chest. He smelled wonderful—a combination of soap, shampoo and a spicy hint of aftershave. His body felt warm and solid, and her breasts tingled with a need to be touched.

She went up on her tiptoes, raising her face for a kiss. With a muffled groan he lifted her off the ground. Cupping her bottom with his big hands, he urged her to wrap her legs around his waist. He leaned down and kissed her until her head spun as if he were turning in a circle, going faster and faster and faster. She clung to his shoulders, accepting all the passion he had to give and giving back everything she could.

It was raw. Exciting. It was…fun. Lord, she'd denied her desire for him for so long, and now that she'd decided to give in to it, she was nearly frantic to get on with the lovemaking.

She wanted to rip off his clothes and see his body. To touch him everywhere. To kiss him until they were both senseless. To make love with him to the point of exhaustion. And utter satisfaction.

She grabbed at his shirt and started yanking the tails out of his jeans. He pulled his mouth away and rested his forehead against hers, breathing almost as hard as he had after the race.

"Are you really sure you want this, sweetheart?"

"Yes." She slid her hands through his thick hair. "Oh, yes. Hurry."

Tightening her legs around his waist, she rubbed herself against the bulge under his fly and sealed his mouth with a kiss that had him groaning. He probably thought she was a sex fiend.

If he did, it didn't put him off any. Kissing her as if he were dying of thirst and she were a cool mountain spring, he carried her to the sofa and sat down with her straddling his lap. He peeled off her tank top in one smooth motion and simply looked at her bare breasts for so long that she nearly lost her nerve and covered them with her arms.

"I knew you'd be beautiful." Using both hands, he touched her with a gentle reverence, tracing the sides, circling her nipples until they contracted into hardened peaks, lifting the rounded flesh with his thumbs.

He raised her up onto her knees and lowered his mouth to her pouty nipples. She arched her back in pleasure as he licked and then suckled them. Fire streaked to a sensitive spot between her legs. As if reading her mind, he lowered one hand and caressed her through her shorts and panties, and she cried out at the momentary relief.

Before she could draw a full breath, he slid his fingers under the hem of her flimsy shorts, then under the silk of her panties. Trembling with anticipation, she waited for his touch, and when it came, the fire returned. Her body moistened his fingertips, and they both made greedy sounds deep in their throats.

Suddenly, all she could think about was getting him naked and touching him the way he was touching her. She pushed him back against the sofa. Kissing him again, she fumbled and tugged at the buttons on his shirt.

One by one they came free, and at last she delved inside, tracing the muscles across his broad shoulders with her palms, combing the wiry patch of hair in the center of his chest with her fingers, lightly raking his lean flanks with her nails. He gasped and flinched as if ticklish. Making a mental note to check that out later, she went to work on his belt and the button at the waistband of his jeans.

While Jack delighted in her eager participation, it

had been so long since he'd made love that he was
afraid of losing control if she didn't slow down. But
she was so quick, her hands so clever and relentless,
and they felt so fantastic on his skin, he hated to interfere with what she was doing. Finally he wrapped
his arms around her, turned to one side and flipped
her onto her back. Leaning over her, he took the clip
from her hair and watched the long, golden strands
tumble to her shoulders.

She looked up at him, her eyes a luminous green,
her cheeks flushed, her mouth swollen from his
kisses. Everything about her was small and sleek and
perfectly in proportion. From her pretty, pink-tipped
breasts to her narrow waist and the sweet, womanly
curving of her hips, she was a warm, living model of
femininity. She was incredibly fit, even strong for her
size, but compared to him, she seemed frighteningly
delicate.

Giving him a tremulous smile, she drew her index
finger from his sternum, down the center of his chest,
past his navel and all the way to the unfastened button
on his jeans. "I won't break."

"Do you read minds?"

"Absolutely." She swung her feet over the side of
the sofa and slid to the floor, holding out her arms to
him. "Come down here. It won't feel so awkward
when you don't have to bend over to reach me."

He did what she'd suggested and discovered she
was right. Lying face to face erased their height dif-
ferential, and his wavering confidence returned. No
matter how long it had been since the last time, this
wasn't something a man forgot.

He gave her deep, wet kisses while he slowly
peeled off her shorts and panties. She was smooth and

satiny soft everywhere, and he lost himself in a tactile exploration of her curves, her hair, her most private places. Stroking her ultrasensitive button of flesh with his thumb, he slid his middle finger inside her. She was moist and tight, and her inner muscles clamped down on him so hard, his mind reeled with possibilities.

And all this time, she was removing his clothing, too, touching him with the same degree of intimacy, exploring his body with the same delight in her eyes that must be glowing in his own. She draped her leg over his hip and wrapped herself around him until they were skin to skin, heart to heart, breath to breath.

With his last vestige of sanity, he pulled away long enough to find his jeans, take out a strip of condoms he'd bought on his way to her apartment and roll one into place. Having watched this procedure with obvious interest, she turned onto her back and opened herself to him. Animal instincts roared through him. Kneeling between her thighs, he positioned himself at the opening to her body and pushed himself inside with a slow, steady pressure, trying to be gentle but desperately wanting to thrust.

She uttered a soft gasp. He froze, then asked in a raspy voice he barely recognized as his own, "Does it hurt?"

"It's been a long time and you're awfully...big. It'll be fine in a second."

Holding himself still was an exquisite form of torture, but he did it. His reward came a few moments later. Her muscles relaxed, and she put her legs around him, crossing her ankles at the small of his back. Flexing his hips, he pushed forward until he reached...paradise.

Gazing into his face, she saw his eyes go glassy and then close tightly as he slid all the way inside her. She felt full, absolutely stretched to the limit, as if she had one foot in the land of pleasure and the other foot in the land of pain. She couldn't move, could barely breathe, but she trusted with every instinct she possessed that in a few moments she would find outrageous satisfaction in his arms.

With agonizing slowness, he started to move, withdrawing a millimeter at a time and then surging back inside her the same way. Her muscles gradually relaxed and her body stretched to accommodate his size. He moved faster, pushed harder, ignited sparks of excitement that blossomed into a fire of pure pleasure, its flames leaping from one nerve ending to another.

Arching her back, she grabbed his hips, dug her fingernails into his rump and strained to meet him at every thrust. Suddenly all sensation telescoped down to the place where their bodies were joined. The pleasure became an excruciating tension, and they both cried out; then it exploded outward in concentric circles of energy that sent her flying.

Only dimly aware of his hoarse shout of completion, she slowly came back to herself. Though he supported most of his weight on his elbows, his head lay heavily on her breasts and his heaving chest and lower body pinned her to the carpet. Loving it, she struggled against limp-noodle muscles to stroke his hair.

She felt his mouth curve into a smile against her bare skin, heard a low, rumbly chuckle. Raising his head, he gave her a grin that made him look supremely satisfied with himself. As well he should. After taking her to the sexual equivalent of heaven, he could strut around, beat on his chest and yell like Tarzan if it would make him happy.

"You're wonderful," she murmured, tracing his eyebrows with her index fingers.

His grin gentled into a tender smile. He caressed her cheek with the backs of his fingers, then leaned down and gave her a kiss so sweet and loving, it nearly brought tears to her eyes.

Drawing back, he said, "You're the one who's wonderful. I could easily fall in love with you."

Chapter Eleven

Abby arrived at Erin's house at five-thirty the next morning, dressed for a run. She desperately needed to talk to her friend before seeing Jack again, and this was probably the only time her friend would be able to squeeze a visit into her busy schedule. Though Erin was slower than Abby, they ran together whenever they could. As expected, Erin came out of her front door ten minutes later, smiling when she saw Abby.

"Hi," she said. "Gorgeous morning, isn't it?"

Abby really hadn't noticed, but to appease Erin's need for pleasantries, she said, "Yes," and fell in step beside her. As usual, they walked two blocks to warm up, then broke into an easy jog.

When they found the right rhythm, Erin glanced at Abby. "What's up?"

Abby didn't even think about stalling. "I've done something terrible."

"Really?"

Abby scowled at Erin's amused, disbelieving smile. "Yes, really."

"What did you do?"

"I made love with Jack last night."

Erin's head whipped around and she almost stepped in a pothole. "What?"

"You heard me. And watch where you're going."

Erin glanced at the ground, then looked back at Abby and grinned. "So, was it good for you?"

"Erin!"

"You're right. Dumb question. If it wasn't good, you wouldn't be in such a snit now."

Explicit memories from the night before flashed through Abby's mind. She shook her head to dispel them, but it didn't help much. "It was better than good. It was fantastic. On a scale of one to ten, it was a fifteen."

"Oh, my," Erin murmured. "Listen, I'm not sure what you want from me here, Abby."

"Advice. What else?"

Looking away, Erin cleared her throat. Abby suspected that she was trying not to smile or laugh. In a month or two, she might laugh herself, but she wasn't there yet.

"You're both single, consenting adults," Erin pointed out. "Could you tell me why making love with him was such a terrible thing to do?"

"Because I'm in love with him, dammit."

"How does he feel about you?" Erin asked, after clearing her throat again.

"Who knows?" Abby rolled her eyes. "He said he could easily fall in love with me. Can you believe that?"

"That depends. Did he say it before or after you made love?"

"After," Abby grumbled. When Erin cleared her throat for a third time, Abby's temper snapped. "Have you got a stupid frog down there or what?"

"A what?"

"A frog. In your throat. Oh, just go ahead and laugh before you choke." She took off at race speed, leaving Erin sputtering behind her. She ran as if hideous demons were chasing her. A mile later, she could still feel them dogging her steps and she realized she could never outrun them. Making a wide *U*-turn, she retraced her route to find Erin.

Good friend that she was, Erin greeted her with a smile. "Feel better now?"

"Not really. I'm so confused, I don't know what to think. Tell me what to think."

Chuckling, Erin shook her head. "Come on, you know it doesn't work that way. I can tell you what *I* think, but I can't tell *you* what you should think."

"Fine. Do it."

"All right. First, you need to take a really deep breath and stop freaking out."

"Easy for you to say."

"Hush up, Abby. I'm serious about this. I've gotten to know Jack fairly well since I've started treating Kitty, and I like him a lot. If you want a man in your life, you could do a lot worse. The question is, do you *want* a man in your life?"

"That's not the right question." Abby started up the "butt" hill, named for its steep slope that worked certain important muscles as a runner struggled her way to the top. "The right one is, what the heck was

I thinking? How could I let myself get so involved with him when I know nothing can come of it?''

Erin stopped and panted for breath. ''Have you told him about your infertility?''

''Of course not.''

''Then, how do you know nothing can come of your relationship?''

Abby came back down the hill to wait until Erin was ready to go on. ''Get real. He's a great father. He's probably going to want more children.''

''He might,'' Erin agreed, ''but he might not. He might feel that Kitty's enough. Or he might be willing to adopt other children. There are options.''

''Oh God, Erin, I know what you're going to suggest, and I can't tell him. I'm just not brave enough—''

''Yes, you are.'' Erin started up the hill again. ''Do you really love him?''

''So much it makes my stomach hurt.''

''I don't need to ask about Kitty. You fell in love with her the first day she walked into your class.''

Blinking back tears, Abby nodded. ''She's exactly what I always imagined my own daughter would be like.''

''She would accept you as her mother without reservation, Abby. I know she would.''

''I suppose so. And I love being with both of them, together or apart. It doesn't matter. Anytime I'm with them it's wonderful. Until I remember it can't last.''

''You still don't know that it can't. Not every man is like Tad or your father. Contrary to female popular wisdom, there *are* some wonderful, mature men in this world. I believe Jack could be one of them.''

''But what if he…rejects me, too?''

"Then, you don't want him because he's a big, stupid loser."

"Oh, right." Abby huffed in disbelief. "The man could have anyone he wanted. He shouldn't settle—"

"But what if he only wants *you?*" Erin demanded. "What if he *doesn't* reject you?"

"Erin—"

"No, forget the excuses. I know this scares you out of your wits."

"You're darn right it does."

"And it's understandable. But can you walk away from Jack and Kitty without ever knowing for sure what he would have said if you'd told him you can't have children?"

"I don't know." Abby sighed and wiped her forehead with the back of one hand. "Dammit, this wasn't supposed to happen. I just wanted to have a pretend family for a few weeks and help Kitty get well. I never thought it would get messy."

They'd reached the top of the hill. Crossing her arms over her midriff, Abby turned around and looked out over Erin's subdivision. The houses were big and well-tended, with beautiful lawns, basketball hoops and lots of minivans and SUVs parked in the driveways. This whole area was a family zone, and she was a single unit who didn't belong here.

Tad's rejection would be nothing compared to how she'd feel if Jack rejected her. He was much more mature than Tad ever would be, and he already had Kitty, so maybe he *could* live with her infertility. But if he couldn't? Could she live with that knowledge, without becoming completely cynical and bitter toward men?

With the sun climbing above the eastern horizon, painting the homes with a pale golden light, she felt lonelier than she'd felt the day her daddy had left because her mother couldn't give him the son he'd always wanted. Lonelier than she'd felt the day her own husband had left her for the same reason. Lonelier and more isolated by her own fears and failings than she'd ever felt in her life.

Erin wrapped her arm around Abby's shoulders. "Come on, Abby. We've talked about this before. You know your worth as a woman and as a human being doesn't depend on having a uterus."

"I know that. I dealt with it a long time ago."

"It doesn't sound like you're quite finished."

"Yes, I am. That's why I have my future planned around my career. That's the most important thing in my life. It's all I can really count on."

"But you didn't make love to your career last night. And as great as your new career might be, it's not going to keep your feet warm at night, or kiss you awake in the morning. Now that you know how good you can be together, Jack is important to you, too. You can't just ignore what happened."

"Yeah, I know," Abby agreed. "But I don't want to be one of those women who sacrifices her own goals and dreams for the sake of having a man."

"Don't make this an either-or situation. You might have to make some compromises, but you don't have to give up your whole career to be with Jack." Erin paused, then added, "Whatever you decide to do, your career will still be there, and so will I. You can call me day or night if you need me."

Abby took a ragged breath, then squeezed the hand

Erin had hanging over Abby's shoulder. "Thanks. Let's go home."

They started jogging again. Neither spoke until they reached Erin's house. Stopping in the street beside the driveway, Erin asked, "Have you decided anything?"

Abby nodded. "I'll see him tonight, and if I can find the nerve, I'll tell him. And we'll see what happens."

"I'm proud of you, Ab." Erin smiled. "And I'll be sending a thousand good thoughts your way, so don't you dare forget to call me."

"I won't." Abby climbed into her Bronco and drove off, wishing that just this once she could be like other women.

Jack's phone rang as he was getting out of the shower. Grabbing a towel, he rushed to answer it. The instant he recognized Abby's voice, he was assaulted by vivid memories of the night before, and his body reacted accordingly.

"Good morning, sweetheart," he said. "Are you missing me as much as I'm missing you?"

She made a strangled sound that he interpreted as agreement, then asked, "Will Millie be staying over again tonight?"

"She sure will," he said with a smile. "I could take Kitty home right after work, and we could go out to dinner. Alone."

Abby hesitated. "I hate to disrupt her routine two days in a row, but I do want to see you alone tonight. What I had in mind was that after you took her home and put her to bed, maybe you could come back. If you don't mind, of course."

Jack laughed. "Mind? If you hadn't called me, I would've called you the minute I got dressed."

"You're not dressed?" There was a funny little squeak in her voice that made him grin like a fool.

"Not a stitch. You caught me coming out of the shower. And I'm missing you terribly." He thought she muttered something with the word *insatiable* in it. And if that wasn't the old pot calling the kettle black…Lord, what a woman she was.

"I've got to get busy," she said, intruding on his momentary fantasy. "I'll see you after work."

"All right. I'll bring dinner. Save some energy for me."

Jack went through his day feeling great. His work went well. His co-workers were less cranky and more helpful. He won an important motion in court. His secretary even caught him whistling and asked if he was all right.

And it was all because of Abby.

By the time he made it to her apartment that evening, he didn't know if he could stand to wait until Kitty went to bed before he had Abby in his arms again. During dinner Abby acted a little jumpy and anxious, too, and he guessed she must be feeling the same way. Luckily, she'd completely worn Kitty out, and it didn't take long to get her settled for the night.

Heart pounding with anticipation, he raced back to Abby's apartment. The instant she let him in, he scooped her into his arms, kicked the door shut and kissed her with all of the passion and longing that had been building inside him since he'd made love to her the last time. She kissed him back with equal fervor.

Eventually, they had to come up for air. He set her

on her feet and she stepped back, one hand clasped to her chest as she eyed him with a wary smile.

"Jack, there's something we need to talk about."

"Hey, I'm sorry," he said. "I didn't mean to jump you like that. I'm not a complete oaf."

"I never thought you were." She led him to the sofa. He sat close beside her and held out his hand. She put her palm on his, linking their fingers. For the first time all day, he felt whole.

"Well, I acted like one. It's just that last night was so great. You weren't the only one who hadn't made love in a long time, you know."

Her eyes widened. "Are you serious?"

"Yeah," he said, nodding. "And I'd only been with one other woman before. I dated Gina all the way through high school and I never wanted anyone else until I met you."

"I don't know what to say."

"You don't have to say anything. I just wanted you to know I consider what we shared last night to be…special. It mattered to me."

"That's so sweet of you."

Her eyes took on a misty sheen, and she swallowed as if she had a lump in her throat. Jeez, the last thing he'd meant to do was make her cry. Panic licked at the corners of his mind. Releasing her hand, he turned to face her, cupping her cheeks with his palms. "What did you want to talk about?"

She looked up at him, her eyes huge and troubled. Even fearful? Of him?

"I, um…I—" she stammered.

"Take your time," he said, encouraging her with a smile.

She nodded, took a deep breath and opened her

mouth, but no words came out. A tear trickled down her cheek, and he caught it with his lips, then pulled her onto his lap and into his arms.

"Shh, babe, please don't cry." He rubbed her back and found her muscles rigid. She was so small that he could span her whole back with one hand. "We'll work it out. It's okay."

She wrapped her arms around his neck and buried her face in his shoulder. He rocked her gently, wondering if he'd offended her by talking about his wife just now. Oh, yeah, that was *real* smooth of him. How could he be such an idiot?

Or maybe Abby didn't want to make love with him again because…hell, he couldn't think of a reason. They'd been fantastic together last night, and that wasn't just his ego talking. He'd heard her cries of satisfaction, felt the involuntary contractions of her inner muscles.

He buried one hand in her hair. "Tell me what's wrong. Whatever it is, I swear, I'll fix it."

She shook her head, then raised it, revealing more tears and a shaky smile. "It's not something you can fix. Just make love to me again."

"But—"

She lay two fingers across his mouth and whispered, "Please, Jack. Make love to me."

He studied her face for clues to her distress, but couldn't find any. Maybe she needed the reassurance of making love again to believe she hadn't imagined how good it had been.

"We'll talk later?"

"Yes," she replied softly.

Sliding one hand under her knees, he got up and carried her into her bedroom. They hadn't made it this far before, but using a bed instead of the floor was bound to be more comfortable, and he wanted this time to be even better. If that was possible.

He lay her on the bed and stretched out beside her. Kissing her deeply, he slowly undressed her and then himself. She turned to him fiercely eager, kissing and caressing him as if this would be the last time they would ever make love. It was all he could do to stay in control, but he managed.

Last night had been about urgency. Tonight was about savoring. Moving with deliberate slowness, he kissed and tasted her from her lips to her heels, lingering at the dips above her collarbones, her breasts, her navel, the insides of her elbows, the backs of her knees and all of her toes, one by one before he worked his way up her legs to the sensitive place that had been his goal all along.

She arched halfway off the bed when he touched her there with the tip of his tongue. He loved her responsiveness. Parting the soft folds between her legs he tasted her again and again, using different amounts of pressure, varying the speed, nearly losing himself in the pleasure of driving her to fulfillment.

While she was still trembling, he put on a condom and thrust himself inside her. The sensations were so intense, he feared his heart might stop beating altogether. She wrapped her legs around his waist, raised herself up on her elbows and licked the side of his neck, then nipped it with her teeth. A violent shiver raced over him, sweeping away his restraint.

He fastened his mouth to hers and started moving, his heart slamming against his rib cage, his blood pumping harder with each thrust of his hips. She clung to him, urging him on with lusty words and exuberant cries. He was holding on to his control by a thread when her inner convulsions started, clamping down on him with rhythmic squeezes until he lost it and collapsed into her welcoming arms.

Rolling onto his side so he wouldn't squash her, he gathered her close. He ran his fingers through her hair, feeling incredibly happy and relaxed and possessive as hell. She was already his woman in every way that mattered. Now all he had to do was convince her of that.

"I told you a lie last night," he said quietly. She started to pull away, but he chuckled and wouldn't let her go. "Now, wait a second, it wasn't a bad lie."

"What other kind is there?" she asked.

"Well, there are little white lies. They're not meant to hurt anyone, really."

She gave him one of those teacher scowls that never failed to tickle him. "What did you lie about, Jack?"

"When I told you I could easily fall in love with you, I was really just testing the waters."

"Jack—"

"Let me finish," he said, shutting her up with a quick, hard kiss. "The truth is, I've already fallen in love with you. I want to marry you and raise Kitty with you, and have more children with you. We'd be so happy together."

"No." She pushed him away with surprising strength. She got off the bed and started grabbing her clothes and putting them on as she found them.

He sat up and watched her for a moment, trying to figure out what in the world was going on. "What do you mean, no?"

"I mean stop building this into a big, romantic fantasy." She looked straight at him, green fires blazing in her eyes. "It was just sex, Jack."

"I don't believe that." He started yanking on his own clothes. "You're not like that, Abby."

She dropped her gaze from his and he saw her throat work down a swallow. "You don't have a clue what I'm really like." She pulled her shirt on over her head and freed her hair with one hand. "I told you a long time ago that I'm married to my career. I'm moving to Portland next month, remember?"

"Okay, maybe my timing's a little off, but we can figure this out."

"There's nothing to figure out." She still wouldn't look at him. "Just drop this crazy idea before you ruin everything."

He zipped his fly, then grabbed his shirt and put it on. "I can't believe you really think it's a crazy idea. You adore Kitty. Anyone who sees the two of you together knows that."

"Yes, I adore her." Now she turned her back on him, and he knew she was hiding something. "That doesn't mean I want to be a mother twenty-four-seven. Did it ever occur to you that I might actually like giving her back at the end of the day?"

"No. I don't know what's going on here, Abby, but you're lying to me."

She glared at him over her shoulder. "How dare you?"

"I'm a professional when it comes to spotting liars. I've seen some really good ones in action, but you're not even close to being good at it." He straightened to his full height and used his best interrogation tone. "Is this about what you wanted to discuss when I first got here?"

"Forget it." Looking pale and agitated, she walked out of the room.

Convinced he was on to something, he scooped up his shoes and socks and followed her. She stood near the front door, arms folded over her chest, one foot crossed over the other in an obvious and unsuccessful attempt to appear casual. He plopped himself down on her sofa and took his time putting on his socks.

"I distinctly remember you saying there was something we needed to talk about. What was it, Abby?"

"It's not important."

Like hell it wasn't. "Is it about Kitty? Has all of this tutoring and keeping her physically active become a burden to you?"

"Of course not—"

A pained expression flitted across her face, nearly breaking his heart.

"—but we did agree that we would start breaking in a replacement by now. For her sake, you need to hire somebody."

"Okay. You've already gone way beyond the boundaries of our original agreement. Get me a list of candidates, and I'll start calling tomorrow."

"I'll fax one to your office."

He finished putting on his shoes and stood up. "All right, now that we've exhausted our business arrangement, let's get back to the subject. What did you want to talk about, Abby?"

"I don't even remember now. Must not've been important. I'll be over to pick up Kitty at the regular time tomorrow. Let's just pretend all of this never happened and go back to being friends. All right?"

"No. I'll always be your friend, but there's no way I'm ever going to forget making love with you."

He slowly crossed the room, keeping his eyes on her face, searching for any indication of what she was thinking. The only emotion he could detect was sadness, but there was a weariness in her eyes that convinced him it wouldn't do any good to keep hammering at her. Dammit, she was hurting, and he was only making it worse.

Stopping beside her, he reached out and tucked a stray lock of hair behind her ear. "I'll leave you alone for now, but this isn't over, Abby. We'll talk about it again later."

He leaned down and kissed her cheek, then opened the door and let himself out, shaking his head in confusion. They'd been fantastic together, but she was desperately trying to pull away from him. Why wouldn't she tell him what was wrong?

Chapter Twelve

Abby stared at the door Jack had just walked through and quietly closed behind himself, her eyes burning with tears and her throat closing around what felt like a five-pound lump of coal. Oh God. The best thing that had ever happened to her had just walked out, his eyes filled with pain.

Pain she had intentionally inflicted.

If he never spoke to her again, it would be no more than she deserved. She reached out and touched the door with trembling fingers, desperately wanting to call him back. Start over. Do whatever it took to make things right between them.

Dammit, she'd been thinking about this meeting all day, even rehearsing what she'd say, but she hadn't handled it at all well. In fact, she didn't see how she could have handled it any worse. She was a sniveling coward.

It was just sex, Jack.

Even while those awful words had been coming out of her mouth, she couldn't believe she was actually saying them. No matter how badly this situation ended, she would always love him for knowing she was lying about that. Jeez, had she ever been lying.

He wasn't going to let her get away with it, either. He was going to dig and poke and prod until she told him everything. Oh, she'd planned to do it, but he'd been so exuberant and so loving and unbearably sweet, when the moment of truth had come, she simply hadn't been able to get the words out of her mouth.

She'd hoped that maybe, after they made love, she would be able to tell him. But then he'd started talking about marriage and having more children, and she'd lashed out at him in fear and pain. All she'd been able to think about was getting him out of her apartment before she fell apart.

Jack was a kind, compassionate man. Now that he'd already said he loved her and wanted to marry her, she feared he would feel compelled to go through with it, even after she told him she couldn't give him more children. Lord, what a mess.

She would rather have him hate her than feel obligated to her, or, worse yet, pity her.

The rest of the night passed in an eternity of self-recrimination and if-I'd-only-saids. She slept through most of her writing time the next morning, and arrived at Jack's house to pick up Kitty feeling as if her batteries badly needed a fresh charge.

Of course, that meant Kitty was bursting with energy. She wanted to go Rollerblading *and* play on the big jungle gym at the park *and* go swimming. By the time Abby managed to drag the kid into the apartment, settle her at the kitchen table and get her started on the day's work sheets, Abby's patience was shredded and a vicious headache snarled a warning just behind her right eye.

Craving a moment's peace, she went into her bedroom and sat at her computer desk. The fat stack of crisp white pages that was all but the last section of her dissertation caught her attention. She ran her thumb up one of the corners, relishing the zipping sound and the feel of the flipping pages, the sense of accomplishment that touching her completed work gave her.

Acting on sheer impulse, she picked up the cordless phone and dialed Dean Kaufman's office in Portland. A secretary answered, and when Abby asked to speak with him, the woman said, "I'm sorry, but he's on vacation until August fifteenth. Is there something I can help you with?"

Abby uttered a soft laugh. "Nothing that can't wait. I was just sitting here and realizing it had been a long time since I'd spoken to him."

"He'll be terribly sorry he missed your call," the secretary said. "Have you set a date for your move to Portland?"

"Not yet," Abby replied. "I haven't found a place to live down there, either. Could you suggest some convenient, reasonably priced areas I should check out?"

"My niece is an excellent real estate agent. Would you like me to have her call you?"

"That would be great," Abby said.

"I'll do that, then," the secretary said. "And please, let us know when you're planning to move.

The other members of the department are anxious to get acquainted.''

"I am too." Abby glanced at her calendar. "Right now, it looks like I'll be moving somewhere between the fifteenth and twentieth of August. Thanks for your help.''

Reassured that her new life was still waiting for her, Abby hung up the phone and stood to leave. When she turned toward the doorway, she discovered Kitty standing just inside the room. Her face looked deathly pale. Her eyes looked big as silver dollars. Her body nearly vibrated with tension. Or was it anxiety? Had she heard that phone call?

"Kitty?" Abby cautiously crossed the room. "What's the matter, sweetie?"

"You're going to go away?" Kitty whispered.

"Not just yet," Abby said, kneeling beside the little girl. "I'll still be in Spokane for about three more weeks."

"Nooooo," Kitty wailed, her voice high and shrill, her eyes oddly vacant. "Don't leave me, Ms. Walsh. Please, don't leave me."

The hair on the back of Abby's neck and on her forearms prickled with alarm. "It's all right, Kitty."

Tears suddenly gushed down Kitty's cheeks and great, heaving sobs shook her whole body. "No, it's not. You can't leave me, too. I'll b-be good this time. I p-promise I won't ever be b-b-bad again."

"Oh, honey, I'm not moving because of anything you did. I'm just going to start a new job. You're not bad."

"Yes, I am bad." Kitty nodded violently and the tears continued to flow. "I'm really, really bad. But

I'll be good this time, Mommy. I promise I'll be good forever. Just don't l-leave m-me.''

Choking on a sob of her own, Abby picked Kitty up and carried her to the bed. She settled the child on her lap and held her close. ''Kitty, what did you mean when you said you'd be good 'this time'?''

''I will. I promise. I know you went away because I was a bad girl, but I won't never do that again.''

Abby rocked Kitty and stroked her hair. ''When were you bad?''

''When you went away, Mommy. I was real bad that day, but I won't never do it again. I love you, Mommy. An' I've missed you so much.''

Sliding around the corner of the bed with Kitty still on her lap, Abby grabbed the phone again and punched the speed-dial for Jack's office. When she told his secretary she needed Jack to come to her apartment right away, the woman sputtered and fumed and said he was in a meeting.

''Then, get him out of the meeting,'' Abby snapped. ''I'm baby-sitting his daughter and she's having a crisis. He needs to be here *now*.''

The instant Abby hung up the phone, Kitty started shrieking. ''No, please. Don't tell my daddy I was bad. He won't love me anymore and he'll go away, too, and then nobody will ever want me.''

''Kitty, sweetheart, calm down,'' Abby begged. ''Your daddy will *always* love you. You are the most precious thing in his whole life and nothing will ever change that.''

''But he loved M-Mommy, too. An' he'll be real m-mad if he finds out she left because of m-me.''

''She didn't leave because of you, Kitty. She couldn't help it. She just died.''

"Nooooo," Kitty insisted. "She wanted me to get in the car and go to play group, but I didn't wanna go."

"What happened then?"

"I was bad. She tried to make me get in the car, and I yelled and I cried and I throwed Mrs. Lady in the flowers."

"Kitty, lots of children do things like that. It doesn't mean you're bad."

"Uh-*huh*." Kitty raised her head from Abby's shoulder and looked at her from haunted, streaming eyes. "Mommy tried to pick me up, and I ran away from her and tried to find Mrs. Lady."

"I see," Abby said. "Then what happened?"

"Mommy grabbed me and put me in the car. We went to the play group house and she didn't even hug me when she left. She never did that before, not ever. And then she never came back to get me. She never came back at all."

"But that wasn't because of you, Kitty. I know she felt just as sad as you did when she left you that day. If she hadn't died, she would have come back for you, and she would have hugged the stuffing right out of you and she probably would've taken you out for a treat so you could make up with each other."

Kitty's red, swollen eyes widened with what looked like hope. "Do you really think so?"

"Oh, I know so. I can tell you had a very good mommy. And sometimes even good mommies like yours feel angry with their children. But they don't stay angry for very long, Kitty. They would never, ever leave and not come back over one little tantrum. And that's all you had."

"Are you sure, Ms. Walsh?"

"Absolutely. Your mommy forgave you before she even got back to her car, honey."

There was frantic pounding on the apartment's front door. Abby went to answer it, carrying Kitty on one hip. As soon as the dead bolt slid back, Jack burst into the room, his tie askew, his hair standing up in patches as if he'd repeatedly run his hands through it, his eyes wild and frantic.

"Where's Kitty?" he demanded. "My God, what happened?"

"She's all right," Abby said, turning to let him see his daughter.

Kitty hid her face behind Abby's shoulder, but Jack didn't seem to notice. He grabbed her around the waist and hauled her into his arms, holding her as if he would never let her go. Kitty started crying again, burying her face against his neck. Jack shot Abby a stricken look that said, *What the hell is going on here?*

Abby stepped closer and patted Kitty's back. "It's all right, honey. Your daddy loves you, no matter what."

"Well, of course I do," Jack said indignantly. "That's what daddies are for. What happened?"

"Kitty, do you want to tell your daddy what happened?" Abby asked. "Or do you want me to tell him for you?"

Kitty shook her head violently. "No, please don't tell. He won't love me no more."

Jack's eyes filled with horror, and he clutched his daughter even tighter. Abby motioned for him to sit on the sofa. He moved in that direction and cautiously settled on the cushions.

"That can't happen, Kitten," he said. "I was there

the day you were born. I loved you from the first second I ever saw your little face, and nothing will ever change that, baby.''

Kitty sobbed piteously. Abby found a pen and a scrap of paper and wrote Jack a short note, cluing him in on Kitty's belief that she had caused her mother to go away forever because of a tantrum. Standing where Kitty couldn't see her, Abby held the paper up for him.

Jack's eyes widened as he read her message, then turned glassy with unshed tears as the meaning sank in. Tightly shutting his eyes, he kissed Kitty's hair and rocked her back and forth. The anguish etched into the lines on his face started Abby's tears flowing. She went into the kitchen for a box of tissues.

It seemed as if it took Jack forever to convince Kitty to tell him what had happened the day Gina had died. Abby's heart broke for him and for Kitty as the story unfolded in a little more detail this time. The child was practically inconsolable, but through it all, Jack was incredibly loving and patient with her. If she hadn't already fallen in love with this man, Abby knew she would have now.

"Kitty," he said, tucking his finger under her chin and coaxing her to meet his gaze, "have I ever lied to you?"

She slowly shook her head. "I don't think so."

"Then you can believe what I tell you now, can't you?"

"I guess so," she whispered.

"Yes, honey, you can. I promise I would not lie to you about something this important, okay?"

"Okay, Daddy."

"There was something wrong with Mommy's heart

and it suddenly just stopped working. She died from
that, and that's the only reason she didn't come back
for you. Do you understand?''

"I think so,'' Kitty whispered.

"Good. You always need to remember that
Mommy didn't leave because of that one tantrum.
You had other tantrums when you were younger, and
she always forgave you and loved you more than anything in the whole wide world.''

"Even more than you?''

Jack gave the question solemn consideration before
answering. "I'm not sure how to answer that. But you
know, a mommy loves her child differently than she
does a daddy. You were inside Mommy's tummy for
a really long time. You were a real part of her, Kitten.
She used to say you were the best part of her. She
always wanted you to be happy.''

"Did she want you to be happy, too, Daddy?''

"You bet she did.''

"And you loved her?''

"Yes, I loved her very much.''

"Then, how come we don't have any pictures of
her?''

"We have lots of pictures of Mommy.''

"Not where I can see 'em,'' Kitty said. "I can't
hardly even remember what she looked like.''

Jack raised one hip and fished his wallet out of his
back pocket. "I've got one right here, and she just
happens to be holding you, Kitten. Would you like to
see it?''

Kitty took the photograph and studied it reverently,
slowly starting to smile. Then she held it out to Abby.
"Wanna see me and my mommy, Ms. Walsh?''

Abby sat down beside them. Surprised to find her

own fingers trembling, she carefully took the photograph from Kitty. Gina Granger had been a striking woman, tall and willowy, with shiny dark hair and brown eyes like Kitty's. In the photo, Kitty appeared to be about a year old, and Gina held her so they were face to face. They were both grinning, their delight in each other obvious and absolutely beautiful. Abby would bet her doctorate that the photographer who had captured that golden moment had been Jack.

Her heart contracting painfully, she handed the picture back to Kitty. The little girl held it in both hands. After looking at it again, she brought it to her mouth and gave it the softest of kisses before returning it to her daddy.

While he tucked it back into his wallet, she asked, "Where are the other pictures of Mommy?"

"They're in a box in my office at home."

"Can I have one?"

"Of course, you can. You can pick any one you like. Even more than one if you want."

"Why did you put them all away?" Abby asked.

Jack looked at her, his eyes filled with sad memories. "After Gina's funeral, they upset Kitty terribly. It was just too painful for both of us."

Kitty sagged against his chest and let out a jaw-cracking yawn. "Daddy, can we go home now?"

"I guess so, honey," he said.

Abby stood and forced herself to smile. "I'll get her things together for you."

Kitty sat up, her forehead wrinkling with an anxious frown. "Aren't you coming with us, Ms. Walsh?"

"I think you need some time alone with your daddy now," Abby said.

Scrambling off Jack's lap, Kitty ran over and wrapped her arms around Abby's legs. "No, I want you to come home, too."

"Absolutely." Jack got up, tugged off his mangled tie and draped it around his neck. "We need you with us, Abby."

Trapped between Kitty's clinging embrace and Jack's determined gaze, Abby could only nod. But Jack couldn't be more wrong. After what had happened today, their need for her would rapidly come to an end. She had fulfilled her goal of making sure Kitty would be all right. Now there was no logical reason she couldn't—or perhaps it was *shouldn't*—go ahead and move to Portland.

She'd known this was coming, of course. She'd planned for it from the beginning. She'd thought Kitty's breakthrough would be cause for a celebration. Now she could ease out of their lives and move on with her own.

But dear God, it felt as if her heart were splintering into microscopic pieces.

Jack drove home, with Kitty humming quietly in the back seat. Abby had promised to follow him in a few minutes, but he felt distinctly uneasy. Oh, he trusted her to keep her word and show up, but he sensed real trouble brewing with her.

He glanced at Kitty in his rearview mirror and sent up a prayer of gratitude for her breakthrough. Since they finally knew what had been troubling her so deeply, he had every confidence Dr. Johnson could help them resolve any other problems that were bothering Kitty. His relief was huge, almost staggering.

None of this would have happened without Abby.

When he thought back to how reluctant he'd been to follow her advice, he could kick himself. Without her stubborn insistence that he take action, Kitty would still be a pale, skinny, sad little ghost. If he hadn't lost her altogether.

One of the most chilling things he'd learned from Dr. Johnson was that depressed children as young as six had been known to attempt suicide. That statistic had scared him so much, he hadn't been able to consider it for more than a few seconds at a time. But now, with Kitty safely on the road to recovery, he couldn't forget it.

Given the enormity of what Kitty had believed about Gina's death, God only knows what might have happened to the child if Abby hadn't intervened. He knew Abby wouldn't want his undying gratitude, but she had it, anyway. And if, as he suspected, she thought her job was done and she could pull away from him and from Kitty now, he intended to show her how wrong she was.

Kitty's worst crisis might have passed, but they still needed Abby's presence in their lives. They always would. The sooner she accepted that idea, the better.

When he parked in the driveway, Millie came out of the house, her face alight with a happy, relieved smile.

"Abby called and told me the good news," she said, hugging him, and then Kitty. "I took out a lasagna from the freezer for supper, and I'm making cherry cobbler for dessert."

"Thanks, Millie," Jack said, grinning as he started toward the house. Millie's first response to any kind of news, good or bad, always had something to do with feeding people. The lasagna obviously was for him; the cobbler was Kitty's favorite. "Did Abby mention what time she'd be over?"

"She was going to stop at the grocery store and pick up a few things to save me a trip, but it shouldn't take her more than twenty or thirty minutes."

They all went into the kitchen. Jack admired the festive table Millie had already set, then said, "Kitty and I have something important to do. We'll be out soon."

Kitty held his hand as they entered the den. He got the box of pictures out of the closet and set it on his desk, then sat in his swivel chair and lifted Kitty onto his lap. Together they sorted through the photographs one at a time, discussing some, crying over others, reminiscing about the good family times they had shared.

It was the first time he and Kitty simply had talked about Gina like this. He was struck by how healing it was for both of them. Thank heaven, they could move forward again now.

Kitty selected two photographs for her room, a larger copy of the one he carried in his wallet and one of Gina alone. They found some nice frames, put the pictures in and took them upstairs. Abby arrived as they were coming back downstairs.

While Kitty ran to her for a hug, Jack studied Abby's face. She looked calm and composed, but he'd swear she had had a crying jag since he'd seen her a little over an hour ago. He could hardly wait to get done with dinner and put Kitty to bed so he could talk to Abby alone.

When Kitty zonked out and Millie finally went home, he poured two glasses of lemonade and led the way into the family room. Abby followed him at a small but noticeable distance. He set the glasses on a pair of coasters, then turned, took Abby into his arms and held her against him. Though it took her several moments to relax, holding her felt wonderful.

"Thank you," he said. "I'll never be able to repay you for everything you've done for Kitty, but I want to say thank you, anyway."

"Knowing she's going to be okay is thanks enough."

"We've put you through a lot this summer."

"I was glad to help." Abby slid her arms around his waist and rested the side of her head on his chest. "She scared me half to death today when she started getting so upset."

"How did it start?" he asked.

"I think she overheard me talking to someone at the college in Portland and figured out I was talking about moving away."

"Oh." Knowing how Kitty would have felt at hearing that, Jack grimaced. He didn't like it much, either. Abby was too caught up in her story to stop now, however, and he wanted to know everything that had happened before he'd arrived at her apartment.

"She started begging me not to leave, and she called me 'Mommy' a couple of times," Abby said. "For a few minutes there, she really believed she was talking to Gina, and the rest of it just came tumbling out after that."

"It's hard to believe she's been blaming herself for Gina's absence all this time. I told her Mommy had gone to heaven."

"She was too young to really understand the concept of death. And kids are so egocentric, they don't always grasp that things happen without involving them somehow. It's awfully unfortunate she had a tantrum that particular morning.''

Jack sighed. ''Yeah, and if Gina wasn't feeling well, she might not have been very patient with Kitty, either. She was a stickler for good behavior. Kitty usually minded her, though.''

''I'm sure she did,'' Abby said. ''She's a very sweet little girl, but you should talk to Erin about changes in her behavior you might expect once she's really feeling better.''

''You think she'll turn bratty?'' Jack asked, chuckling.

''I doubt it, but she'll probably test the limits more than she did before, and she's liable to argue with you a lot more than you're used to. This is where you'll get to put your negotiating skills to good use.''

''What? I don't get to trot out my mother's old favorite 'Because I said so'?''

''You can always try.'' Abby laughed, then leaned back and looked up into his face. ''But your daughter's way too smart to fall for that.''

''Then it's a good thing you'll be around to help me keep up with her.''

Abby stiffened, then pushed herself out of his embrace. ''It's not going to happen, Jack. I told you that last night.''

''Well, let's talk this out.'' He stepped back, gestured toward the leather sofa. When she'd settled into a corner, he handed her a glass of lemonade and sat on the cushion next to her. ''Do you really want to move to Portland?''

''Would I have gone to all the trouble of getting my doctorate and a new job if I didn't?''

''But that was before you fell in love with me and

Kitty. Doesn't knowing that we love you back and want you to be with us change anything for you?"

"You're not really in love with me," she said.

He frowned at her. "Don't tell me how I feel."

Abby firmly shook her head. "You probably feel like you're in love, but it's really just gratitude and relief over Kitty."

"I know what being in love feels like, and I don't make love with someone out of gratitude and relief. Trust me on that one, will you?"

"Okay, maybe I'm not saying this the right way." She set her lemonade back on the coaster and held out one hand with the palm up, while she touched her sternum with the other hand. "It's not really *me* you're in love with. What you're really in love with is the idea of having a mother for Kitty and a wife to help you raise her. You could easily find lots of other women who would fit your requirements."

"Excuse me?" Her attitude was seriously starting to tick him off. He took a deep breath to calm his rising temper, then took another one for good measure. "Are you saying that just any woman would do, here?"

"You're probably more choosy than that, but surely you realize we make a pretty odd couple. We don't even have that much in common, really."

"That didn't seem to bother you much the past two nights." He stopped and pointed his index finger at her. "And don't you dare say it was just sex again. I'm not buying that one. Period. End of discussion."

"Oh, that's really helpful. It just opens communication right up."

"Are you saying you *don't* love me?" he asked. "Not at all?"

Fresh pain flared in her eyes and she looked away before quietly admitting, "I didn't say that."

"Then why are we arguing, here?"

"Because sometimes love isn't enough to make things work."

"And you think this is one of those times?"

Biting into her lower lip and still not looking at him, she nodded. "I know it is, Jack. And there's nothing either one of us can say or do that will change…things."

"What things?"

"I can never be the wife you really want."

"I thought I was the one who was supposed to decide that," he said, smiling at her when she snuck a glance at him. "From where I'm sitting, you'll do just fine."

"No, I won't. Nadine told me what a perfect lawyer's wife Gina was. How she entertained the right people and served on the right charity boards—and that's not me. I can't do that sort of thing."

"Who asked you to?" Jack wanted to shake her. Dammit, he couldn't believe she was making a big deal about such inconsequential things. "I can understand how you might feel a little funny about Gina after today. You heard a lot about her and you finally got to see what she looked like."

"Exactly. And I'm not even remotely like her."

"So what? I loved Gina with all my heart, and I won't say otherwise for you or anyone else. But you don't have to compete with her or her memory."

"Are you sure of that?"

He turned toward her and took her hands between his. "Abby, my feelings for you are very different from what I felt for Gina, but they're every bit as strong and wonderful in their own way. My whole life is different now. I don't want to go back to the way things were. I'm ready to move on. With you."

"Oh, Jack." Tears welled up in her eyes and his heart sank, but he wasn't ready to give up yet.

"Aw, don't cry, honey."

She yanked her hands back, wrapped her arms around herself and stood, pacing over to the empty fireplace. He got up to follow her, but she shook her head violently and waved him away. "Don't, Jack."

"Don't *what?* Comfort you the way you've comforted me and my daughter for weeks, now? That hardly seems fair."

"Just forget about marrying me." She took a deep, shuddering breath, then let it out. "You're going to have to find someone else."

"I don't want anybody else. I want to marry you and have children with you." He jammed one hand through his hair in frustration. "Why is that so damn hard for you to believe?"

"Because I can't do it," she said, sounding as if she was choking on a sob.

"It feels like we're having two different conversations, and I'm missing something. Will you *please* tell me what it is?"

She covered her face with her hands. "Don't make me say it."

"Abby, you're driving me crazy, here. Whatever it is, I'll fix it. I told you that last night."

"And I told you last night that you *can't* fix it."

"For God's sake, what the hell is so bad that it can't be fixed?"

Her voice came out soft and flat. "I can't have children."

He couldn't have heard that right. "What?"

"I can't have children." She took away her hands and looked straight at him, tears dripping from her chin. "*Now* do you get it?"

"But you're so young and healthy—"

"I had a hysterectomy six years ago."

"Oh, God," he whispered. He hadn't had a clue. Didn't know what to say. Doubted he could get any words out even if he did know what to say.

"Yeah, that's what I thought." She swiped at her eyes with the back of one hand and straightened her spine. "I have to leave."

"Not yet. Give me a minute, and—"

"No, I mean I have to leave Spokane. Now. As soon as I can arrange it."

The determination in her eyes rattled him so much that he blurted out the first thing that came to mind. "You can't leave. Kitty needs you. She depends on you."

"I would never hurt Kitty," she said fiercely. "But it's really in her best interests not to depend on me. I've been telling you that all along."

"But, Abby—"

"I'll talk to Erin," she interrupted. "We'll figure out the best way to handle this. But you and me...it's over, Jack."

She turned and hurried from the room. Stunned by everything he'd heard in the past ten minutes, he just stood there, completely unable to respond, even when he heard the back door slam and the engine of Abby's Bronco roar to life. After a day of such mental and emotional turmoil, he simply couldn't move or even react.

His daughter had come back to him at last, and he was happy—hell, he was ecstatic—about that. But with Abby's departure, he also felt as if his whole life had just exploded and gone straight to hell.

Chapter Thirteen

Jack stayed home from work the next day to be with Kitty. From the moment she came out of her bedroom still wearing her shorty pajamas and demanding breakfast before she "starved right to pieces, Daddy," it was apparent the behavioral changes were already starting. Delighted with her impish grin, he picked her up, held her over his head and spun her around until she shrieked with laughter.

If only Abby were there to see Kitty like this. He thought about phoning her, but decided it might be a good idea to give her a little more time. Every time he thought about what she'd told him, he ached for her. Knew he'd blown it big time last night. Knew he'd hurt her other times, too.

Clear back in May, he'd made some smart remark about her needing to get married and have a kid of her own if she wanted to know how hard it was to be a parent. God only knows how many other stupid things he'd said that he couldn't remember. It didn't matter that he hadn't known the truth back then.

It only mattered that he'd hurt her and he felt like a damn jerk and he didn't know how to repair the wounds he'd inflicted.

He wanted to go to her and tell her he didn't need any more children. He already had Kitty. On the other hand, if they decided they wanted more children, they could always try to adopt some, even if they had to go overseas to do it. But he wasn't sure she was ready to hear that, much less discuss it.

It would be a relief to take some kind of action. But what? Just when it seemed as if happiness was finally within his reach, one wrong move might lose him this special woman he loved so much. If he pushed her too hard or too fast, Abby would run like the wind and be gone for good.

The only hope was to sit tight and wait for her to contact him when she felt ready to talk. In the meantime, he intended to give Kitty tons of attention. Abby had to approve of that.

Dr. Johnson was able to fit Kitty into her schedule that afternoon, and after the session she arranged for her receptionist to watch Kitty while Jack went into the office for a brief visit. The office was small, cozy, and a little too feminine for his comfort. Sitting on a puffy blue love seat, he leaned forward, clasping his hands together between his spread knees. Dr. Johnson gracefully settled into an armchair facing him.

"What do you think?" he asked. "Of Kitty, I mean."

Dr. Johnson's smile reassured him even before she

spoke. "We've still got some work to do, but she's definitely turned the corner."

"She's going to be all right, then?"

"It looks that way. She may slip back a time or two, just to check on whether she gets the same response from you whenever the subject comes up. As long as you consistently reassure her that what happened to her mother wasn't her fault and you love her no matter what, she should be fine. It's a very good thing we caught it now, of course."

He nodded. "I thought about that yesterday. If Abby hadn't gotten on my case, I don't know how long it would've taken me to get Kitty some help. She's a lucky kid to have Abby for a teacher."

"I agree," Dr. Johnson said. "But then, I think any kid who has Abby for a teacher is a lucky kid. Have you heard from Abby today?"

Jack studied Dr. Johnson for a moment. Her tone and manner were casual, but he knew she and Abby were best friends. Just how much did the good doctor know about his relationship with Abby?

"Not yet."

"I haven't, either," Dr. Johnson said. "I was expecting her to call me yesterday, but she didn't."

"Yesterday was pretty emotional for all of us."

"I can imagine." She stood, indicating the end of their visit, but he sensed there was more she would have liked to say to him. "I'll see you and Kitty next week, then?"

"We'll be here," Jack agreed. "Thanks for all your help."

"I'm delighted things are going so well for both of you."

Jack took Kitty to Didier's for frozen yogurt with

"bunches and bunches of sprinkles" on it. He thought about taking some to Abby as a combination peace offering and excuse to check on her, but decided to go home, instead. He could call her and tell her about Kitty's appointment with Dr. Johnson.

Jack tried to focus his attention on Kitty, but Dr. Johnson's question about Abby lingered in the back of his mind. Had she been trying to tell him something indirectly? He thought maybe she had, but he'd never been any good at figuring out a woman's hints.

When he got home, there was a stilted message from Abby on the voice mail, recommending a woman named Patty Spencer as a replacement tutor for Kitty. Jack tried to call Abby back, but she didn't answer her phone. Muttering under his breath in irritation, he phoned Patty and asked her to stop by the next day for an interview.

With that settled, he took Kitty out and bought her a little pink bicycle with training wheels and a safety helmet. It was time for him to take responsibility for his daughter's activities. If she was going to have more energy now, he needed to provide productive ways for her to burn it off.

Abby finally called back just before Kitty's bedtime. She asked to speak to Kitty, and Jack was reduced to listening avidly to the kid's side of the conversation.

"I missed you today," Kitty said. "Are you coming to get me tomorrow?"

Kitty nodded several times in a row, and it bugged him that he couldn't figure out what Abby was saying. Then Kitty grinned.

"Okay. Guess what? Daddy bought me a bike. It's

pink. Uh-huh, it's really pretty, but it has those dumb baby wheels on it.''

Jack leaned down and gave Kitty a scowl that made her giggle.

A moment later, she said, "Okay. I love you, Ms. Walsh. 'Night.''

Kitty handed the receiver to Jack, then scampered out of the room when he told her to put on her pajamas.

Terrified as any teenager, he put the phone to his ear. "Hello, Abby. How are you?''

"I'm fine—''

Aw, jeez, her voice was brisk and businesslike, exactly the way she'd sounded last spring.

"Did you phone Patty Spencer?''

He didn't want to talk about Patty Spencer, for God's sake, but he said, "She's coming for an interview tomorrow.''

"Good. She was my student teacher last year, so Kitty already knows her. If you decide to hire her, I'll show her what Kitty still needs to cover. How is Kitty?''

"She's done really well so far. We had a good visit with Dr. Johnson.''

"I know. I talked to her after your appointment. Now then, I'll be picking Kitty up tomorrow as usual, but then I'm going to be phasing out of the picture as quickly as possible.''

"Phasing out—''

She went right on talking as if he hadn't spoken. "Patty may be willing to take over keeping Kitty busy as well as tutoring her, but if not, you might want to think about hiring a high school or college girl to come and do things with Kitty until school starts. Then you can help her make friends her own age.''

Oh Lord, she had everything all worked out. How to phase herself out of Kitty's life. And out of his. The thought made him sick. ''Abby, can we talk about any of this?''

''Was there something you didn't understand?''

Everything. How can you be so passionate with me one day and act like I'm a stranger the next? Was it just sex, after all? Was I wrong about that? Will you ever be able to forgive me for hurting you?

He wanted to say all of that and more, but as long as she had these barriers up, what was the point?

''No, I guess not.''

She said a brief good-night and hung up. He stared at the handset of his own phone for a moment, then returned it to the base, sadly shaking his head. Oh man, he was in trouble here.

Rather than giving her time to cool off, he should have barged into her apartment while she was still vulnerable and made her listen to him. Unfortunately, he could see that it was already too late to do what he should have done.

While he'd been giving her time, she'd been building unscalable walls around her heart and had locked him out. If he hadn't known she was hurting, he would have been furious with her. Now he just felt panic. But that wouldn't help anything.

He took a deep breath. Then another. He wasn't going to give up on Abby. He couldn't. He promised himself that above all else he would handle this situation like a sane, rational adult.

For five days, he tried everything he could think of to get Abby to have a serious conversation with him, short of having one of his brothers arrest her and handcuff her to his bed. But he was no closer to success, the arrest-and-handcuff scenario was starting to seem like a viable alternative, and he decided that when dealing with someone as stubborn as Abby, acting like a sane, rational adult was highly overrated.

Kitty liked Patty Spencer and seemed to be handling the transition just fine. Jack was the one who was completely miserable without Abby. He'd finally had enough.

This was war.

For his first volley, he went to a florist specializing in roses and spent a hundred dollars on the "I Was a Jerk, Please Forgive Me" bouquet. The florist promised to deliver it within the hour.

He went back to his office and tried to work while he waited for her response, but he couldn't concentrate. His phone rang two hours later. Certain it was Abby, he grabbed it up, only to hear the florist's unmistakable nasal voice.

"Hey, Jack, we have a little problem with your delivery."

"What is it?" Jack asked.

"This Abby Walsh lady's out of town. You want to hold off with this until she gets back?"

"How do you know she's out of town?"

"Her neighbor told the delivery guy. What do you want to do with the flowers?"

"Hold off for now. I'll have to let you know later."

Frustrated to his eyeballs, Jack left work and drove straight to Erin Johnson's office. He arrived just as she was leaving for the day. Obviously surprised to see him, she paused with her key still in the door's lock.

"Jack. Is everything all right?"

"No."

She frowned. "Is it Kitty?"

"It's Abby. I know she talks to you, so please just answer one question. Where is she?"

Erin paused for a moment, studying him with a considering expression that warned him not to mess with her. "Why do you want to know?"

"I intend to marry her."

"Even though she can't have children?"

"Hell, yes."

"Why didn't you say so when she told you about her infertility?"

"It was like a hit-and-run, Erin."

She frowned as if she wasn't sure she believed him. "How so?"

"I was proposing to her. She hits me with this bombshell out of nowhere, and before I can pick my jaw up off the floor, she's telling me she's leaving Spokane—and then she's out the door. I've been patient as a saint, but I haven't been able to get her to talk to me about it once. And now she's left town without even telling me?"

"You sound angry," Erin observed, her tone perfectly neutral.

He hated it when therapists did that. Still, he had to answer her honestly. "I am, dammit." He paused, then added grudgingly, "And I'm scared. She's assuming I'm some jerk who won't love her because she had to have surgery. I don't even know why she had to have it. I've been praying it wasn't cancer—"

"It wasn't," Erin said. "Physically, she's fine now."

"Oh, thank God." He took a couple of deep breaths and wiped his forehead with the back of a shaking hand. "Sorry, I didn't realize how scared I was about that until just now."

"That's all right," Erin said, her tone noticeably warmer. "You really love her, don't you."

He gave her a rueful smile. "What's not to love? I admit I'm pretty irritated with her, but I know something else is going on. She seemed so afraid to tell me she couldn't have kids, and then, once she did, she just *knew* it was all over. Why would she think that?"

"It's not my story to tell," Erin said. "But I can say that she has her reasons."

"Somebody really hurt her," he said grimly. "I thought so. And I did, too, but I didn't mean to. Erin, please, tell me where she is so I can straighten this out."

"You think I'm going to rat out my best friend for you?"

Jack noticed her grin and slowly grinned back. "She'll thank you for it later."

Hot, tired and cranky after a long, unsuccessful afternoon of apartment hunting, Abby drove back to her motel room. In the past three days, she'd looked at thirty apartments in a variety of price ranges. Unfortunately, none of them felt like...home—no, she wasn't going to think about a farmhouse and a little dark-haired girl and a man. Especially not *that* man. She would find a suitable apartment tomorrow.

The ironic thing was, she'd been looking forward to moving to Portland for months, but after only a few days here, she was already having second thoughts. So far the only thing she really liked about the city was not having to pay a sales tax. Compared to Spokane, the traffic was horrendous, the housing prices were much higher, and she felt like a lonely, insignificant grain of sand on a wide stretch of beach.

Looking forward to a shower and a nap, she parked the Bronco behind the motel and hurried through the cool, empty corridors toward her room. She inserted her key in the slot, then let out a startled shriek when a big man suddenly appeared at her side.

"Hello, Abby," Jack said.

Clutching her chest with both hands, Abby glared at him. "Holy Moses, you nearly scared me to death."

"Open the door, Abby."

Lord, but he'd frightened her out of the blessed numbness she'd finally managed to achieve. Any second now, she'd go back to feeling hurt, and she didn't want to do that. She'd much rather feel numb. "What are you doing here?"

"You know what I'm doing here. We have to talk."

If he was feeling anything more than impatience, he was doing a good job of hiding it. "Who's taking care of Kitty?"

"Millie and Patty. Kitty's okay. Open the door."

"How did you find me?"

"Take a wild guess."

She frowned. "Erin told you?"

"You win the gold toaster. Quit stalling and open the door. I'm not leaving until you hear me out."

What was this? He didn't usually use sarcasm with her anymore. She shot him a frosty look, then opened the door and swept inside, turning on every light in the place as she went.

He took his time following her into the room, looking too big for the small space and unbearably dear to her at the same time. He wore navy slacks and a blue polo shirt, and his hair had been freshly cut. There were dark circles under his eyes, but a fierce determination burned in the depths of his gaze.

Her stomach clenched and a fluttering sensation filled her chest. Painfully aware of the queen-size bed filling up half the room, she sidled closer to the small round table and two chairs occupying a corner near the TV. He approached her with a wry smile, as if he knew she was thinking about being alone with him in a motel room.

Unwilling to let him draw out the tense silence any longer, she said, "Let's sit down."

He sat on the side of the bed facing the table and held out one hand, silently suggesting she take one of the chairs. When she was settled, he just sat there looking at her, his eyebrows beetled in perplexity, until she wanted to scream at him.

But this wasn't the nice Jack Granger she'd come to know and love. This was the old Jack Granger, the prosecuting attorney, also known as Granger the Grouch.

"What did you want to say to me, Jack?"

"First, what the hell are you doing here? Running away from me?"

"I'm carrying out the plans I've had all along. I told you about them before I agreed to tutor Kitty."

"What about *us*, Abby?"

"There is no 'us.'"

"Wrong answer. You don't end a relationship like we had that easily."

"I don't know why not. Unless you're planning to stalk me all the way to Oregon?"

That was a cheap shot and she knew it. He waved one hand as if brushing away a remark so ridiculous it didn't deserve a reply. "What did you honestly expect me to do when you told me you couldn't have children?"

"Exactly what the other men in my life did when they heard that news."

"Which was?"

Abby tried to keep the bitterness out of her laugh, but when Jack's gaze sharpened she realized she hadn't succeeded. "Run for the nearest fertile woman they could find and get her pregnant as soon as was humanly possible."

"Who exactly are you talking about? Your ex-husband?"

"He's one of them. My dad's the other one. When the doctor told him my mother wouldn't be having any more children after me, he was out the door so fast, I always think of him as a blur. In some weird way he was ashamed of me and afraid that he'd only be able to father a girl. He eventually married a woman ten years younger than Mom, and they have three grown sons."

Jack's eyes widened. "You have three brothers?"

"Half brothers. I've never met them and I doubt they even know I exist." Abby shrugged, pretending it didn't hurt anymore, but it did. She suspected it always would. His appalled look was a balm to her bruised heart.

"Your dad didn't stay in touch with you?"

"I haven't seen him or heard from him since I was Kitty's age," Abby said. "I only know about his other family because Mom watches for notices about him in the newspaper and then passes on the information whether I want to know or not."

"I'm sorry," he said quietly. "That stinks."

Unable to witness the compassion in his eyes without risking tears, she glanced out the window. "I was better off growing up without him. If he'd stayed with us, I would've been a constant reminder that he didn't have the son he wanted so much. He would've resented me for that."

"That's possible," Jack said. "What did your ex-husband do?"

Furious that this ancient history still had the power to wound her, she turned to glare at Jack. She'd worked hard to put all of this behind her, and he thought he could sit there and calmly demand that she resurrect her most painful memories? "You don't need to know that."

"I disagree. If you're going to reject me based on his actions, I deserve to know what he did. What's his name?"

"Tad," she said. "Tad Carlisle."

"What does he do for a living?"

"I know exactly what you're doing," she told him. "It's an interrogation technique. If one question's too sensitive, you back up and ask a few easy ones before you return to the original one. Right?"

His challenging smile told her he knew her far too well for comfort.

"So humor me and answer the easy ones. What does Tad the Idiot do for a living?"

She almost smiled. How would Jack feel if he knew

she had similar nicknames for him? "He's a software designer."

"How long were you married?"

"Four years. I was eighteen when I married him, just a year out of high school, because I graduated a year early. My mother was not happy about it, but she helped me finish college, anyway."

"She sounds like a nice lady."

"She is," Abby agreed. "She's a little phobic about trusting men, but she's built a good life for herself now."

"I'm looking forward to meeting her," Jack said.

Oh, he thought he was so smooth. And he *was* smooth, Abby admitted, if only to herself. But not quite smooth enough to keep the next logical question from hurting her.

"What happened with Tad?"

Just thinking about Tad made her feel as hollow inside as she'd felt right after the hysterectomy. Hollow, useless, undesirable. Take your pick. Wanting to hide her face from him, she turned her head toward the window again and took slow, shallow breaths. She didn't hear him move, but suddenly he was down on one knee beside her chair, putting his arm around her shoulders, stroking her hair with incredible gentleness.

"Tell me, Ab. You're almost done."

She nodded, then took a moment to collect her thoughts. "I had a medical condition called endometriosis."

"I've heard of it," he said.

"It's unusual for someone as young as I was to have it, and I had an unusually severe case. Even without the hysterectomy, I would've been infertile, but the surgery at least ended the pain and the bleeding.''

''I'm sorry you had to go through that.''

''Lots of people go through much, much worse.'' She shrugged again, gave him a watery smile. ''Tad moved into the guest room when I came home from the hospital. He said he was afraid he'd disturb my rest and that he'd come back to our bedroom when I was well. But by then his assistant at work was already pregnant with their first baby, a little girl. Two years later, they had twin boys. He sent me a Christmas card with a family picture on it so I could see how happy he was.''

Jack muttered a pithy phrase that should have shocked Abby, but somehow made her feel that he was on her side, instead.

''You didn't deserve any of that, sweetheart.''

''I know,'' she said. ''Neither did my mother. But these things happen sometimes, and you have to dust yourself off and go on with your life. That's what I've been doing for the past six years.''

''I admire your spirit,'' Jack said. ''But there's no reason you have to spend the rest of your life alone.''

She hated him for being such a good listener. For being so sweet and understanding and rational. For making her want to believe that it really might be different with him. Most of all, she hated him for forcing her to dig up the strength to turn him down again for his own good as well as her own.

''Don't.'' She pulled away from him and got up, then walked to the bench at the foot of the bed and stood beside it. Crossing her arms over her breasts, she turned back to look at him. ''Don't ask me to marry you again. You don't really mean it.''

"As a matter of fact, I do." He held her gaze for an excruciating moment. "I love you. Nothing's going to change that."

"Jack, please. You feel sorry for me. You feel grateful to me. Whatever. But you aren't in love with me."

"Not true. I love *you,* Abby. Not your uterus."

His eyes would undo her if she kept looking at them. She glanced away, steeled herself to do what needed to be done. "You have 'daddy' written all over you. Both times you talked about marriage, you mentioned having more children in the next sentence. You obviously want them."

"Not if it means losing you," he said.

Abby shook her head at him. "You should've seen the disappointment in your eyes when I told you. You were crushed. Don't even bother trying to deny it."

"I'm not denying anything," he said. "I'd love to have a child with you, and I deserve to feel disappointed that we can't share that experience. But that doesn't mean I don't want you anymore."

"Please—"

His face flushed and temper sparked in his eyes. "Dammit, you've had years to get used to the idea. That night at my house you hit me with this news, and on the basis of a thirty-second, knee-jerk reaction, you tried and convicted me of being like your dad and Tad the Idiot. Was that fair?"

"It doesn't matter if it's fair. None of this has been fair to me, and I just don't have enough faith left to try this again." She sank onto the bench, bowed her head and covered her face with her hands. "You don't understand."

"I've lost people I loved, too," he said.

"It's not the same thing at all. You lost your father and your wife to premature death, and I'm not discounting the pain you felt. But I've lost the two most important men in my life because—" She paused and touched her sternum with her fingers. "Because *I* wasn't what they wanted. *I* wasn't enough to make them happy. I heard it as a child and as a young wife, and it nearly destroyed me."

"Abby, I swear to you, it won't happen again. Not with me."

"I want to believe that. For a little while this summer, I thought maybe I actually could. But I just can't."

"You're not listening to what I'm saying."

"No, Jack. You're the one who's not listening. When Tad left me, I was so depressed, I wanted to die. My mom dragged me to a doctor and a therapist and refused to give up on me. I had to fight like the devil to find something I could believe in again. Something to live for. Something I could count on."

"You're talking about your career," he said.

"That's right. My career is my life now. And as much as I might like to, I can't risk compromising it for you or even for Kitty. If marriage didn't work out between us, I couldn't survive losing both of you. Please, if you really do love me, don't ask me again."

His eyes were noticeably damp, but he held her gaze without trying to hide his tears. "Well, I do really love you, Abby. When you finally get to a place where you can believe that, and you realize that I'm not like your dad or Tad Carlisle, I'll still be waiting for you. But I won't bother you any more right now. I do have to ask you for one favor, though."

"What's that?"

"Before you actually move here, I want you to come and say goodbye to Kitty. She needs to know that you're leaving and that it's not because of her. Will you do that for her?"

"Of course. I'll be glad to do that."

"Thanks. Well, I guess this is it, then."

He walked to her side, pulled her into his arms and took her mouth in a sweet, melancholy kiss that seemed to go on forever. Raising his head, he studied her face and tucked her hair behind her ears.

"You say your career is your life now, but you're not going to get the daily hugs and affection from college kids that you're used to getting from first graders. Do you think your professional relationships will give you the love you need to be happy? Real living is messy and it hurts sometimes, but I've learned to prefer it over simple survival. That's the question you need to be asking now. Do you want to really live—with me and Kitty? Or are you going to settle for survival—with your career?"

Chapter Fourteen

Her heart nearly dragging on the ground, Abby pulled into Jack's driveway on a Friday evening two weeks later. She didn't want to do this but she'd promised Jack she would. There was no way out.

Gathering up her purse and the big, fuzzy bear she'd brought Kitty from Portland, she climbed out of the Bronco and headed for the house. Halfway to the front door she paused to take in the changes she never would have imagined possible the first time she'd come here. The old farmhouse looked warm and welcoming. Like a real home.

Several windows were open. The flower beds rioted with lush green foliage and big colorful blossoms. A yellow plastic water slide still attached to a garden hose was draped over a bush. The pink bike minus the training wheels Kitty had told her about was propped against the front porch.

Climbing the steps to the porch, Abby felt every bit as nervous as she had that night she'd come here with chocolate chip cookies and learning targets. That seemed about right, since this undoubtedly was the last time she'd ever come here.

Well, there was no sense in stalling. Procrastinating wouldn't make saying goodbye to Kitty and Jack any easier.

She jabbed the doorbell with more force than was strictly necessary. An instant later she heard Kitty hollering inside.

"She's here, Daddy. She's here!"

"Let her in," Jack called. "I'll be right there."

There was the sound of small bare feet running across the tile entryway. The door swung open and a dark-haired little imp fairly dancing with excitement grinned at Abby through the screen.

"Hi, Ms. Walsh. Come in. Come in. I've been waiting forever to see you!"

When Abby stepped across the threshold, Kitty threw herself against her legs and hugged her with amazing strength. Dropping her purse and the bear, Abby squatted down and hugged the little girl back, inhaling the sweet scent of shampoo, brushing her cheek against baby-fine hair and relishing the feel of that warm, solid little body against hers.

Lord, how she had missed this child.

Kitty was the first to let go. Abby held on for one more squeeze, then released her. Kitty pounced on the bear and picked it up, rubbing her nose against its soft fur.

Giving Abby a winsome smile, she said, "Oooh, that's a very nice bear."

"I'm glad you like him," Abby said. "I bought him for you, Kitty."

Kitty's eyes widened with the generous dose of drama Abby had suspected might be lurking under all that depression. It would be so much fun to watch this kid's personality bloom like those flowers outside.

"Really? Thanks, Ms. Walsh."

"You're welcome, sweetie."

"We have a present for you, too." Kitty shifted the bear to her left arm and offered Abby her right hand. "Let's go find Daddy."

Abby wanted to say, "Let's not," and run back to her Bronco, but Kitty was already leading her into the living room and Jack was coming in from the family room. He carried a large, flat package, enthusiastically gift-wrapped in white paper and a cluster of green-and-silver bows that might have been left over from Christmas. Giving Abby a lopsided grin that made her heart contract, he came to meet her.

"Abby. It's good to see you." His gaze ran over her from her head to her toes and back again.

She knew how he must be feeling. He looked even better to her now than he had back in Portland. She could drown in the warmth of his eyes, and his smile was a kiss waiting to happen. He had the power to make her feel feminine and sexy and a hundred other wonderful things she hadn't consciously realized she'd been missing until this moment.

"See what Ms. Walsh gave me?" Kitty asked, holding up the bear.

Jack shot her a quick, distracted glance, then returned his gaze to Abby. "It's nice, Kitten. I hope you said thank-you."

"She did," Abby assured him.

"Give her *our* present, Daddy," Kitty said.

"Oh." He looked down at the package in his hands as if he'd forgotten it was there. Turning to Kitty, he said, "You're the one who made it. Why don't you give it to her?"

Kitty rolled her eyes like a put-upon teenager, carried her new bear to a wing chair and set it carefully on the seat. Going back to her father, she took the package from him and gravely handed it to Abby.

It was surprisingly heavy. Fearing she might drop it if she tried to open it while standing up, Abby went to the sofa, sat down, set the package on her lap and patted the cushion beside her.

"Come and help me, Kitty. Did you do this lovely wrapping yourself?"

Nodding, Kitty gave her a proud smile. "I did the bows. Daddy did the rest."

"The rest is lovely, too," Abby said.

"Thanks."

Jack sat on the coffee table, facing her, his knees almost brushing hers. He watched intently while she pulled the paper away from a fire-engine red picture frame. Or rather, the back of a fire-engine red picture frame.

"Turn it over." Kitty eagerly took the edge of the frame and lifted it.

Abby caught it as it came down with the other side up, took one look and felt her breath catch in her chest. "Oh, my," she whispered, gazing through stinging eyes at Kitty's Mother's Day gift, now matted and framed. Abby could still see where some of the wrinkles in the paper had been, but the photo of

Kitty, the poem and the little red handprints brought a lump to her throat.

Kitty got up on her knees and draped her arms loosely around Abby's neck. "Will you keep it this time, Ms. Walsh?"

"I'd be honored to, Kitty. Thank you."

Laying her head on Abby's shoulder, Kitty said, "I don't want you to forget me."

Abby leaned over and kissed the top of Kitty's head. "I could never forget anyone as adorable as you."

Kitty raised her head. "Do you really have to move away?"

"I'm afraid so, honey."

"I wish you wouldn't." Kitty gulped as if she was trying not to cry. "I was hoping you'd marry my daddy and me so you could be my mommy for real and I could make you more stuff for next Mother's Day."

Abby nearly choked on a sob, but managed to get her emotions back under control enough to say, "That's awfully sweet of you Kitty. But you know, in time your daddy will probably find someone else to be your mommy."

Kitty looked her straight in the eye and slowly shook her head. "No, Ms. Walsh. You're the only mommy we're ever gonna want." Her chin trembled, her voice wobbled and a tear trickled down her right cheek. "If you won't marry us, we'll be all alone forever and ever."

Abby hugged Kitty tightly against her, shutting her eyes against the pain tearing her heart apart. Where had she gone so wrong? She'd only wanted to help this precious child, but she'd hurt Kitty as much as she'd hurt Jack and herself.

Jack stood and took Kitty into his arms. She reached back for Abby, but he shushed her and carried her into the family room. Abby heard them talking softly for a moment, then he returned, closing the pocket doors behind him and bringing a box of tissues with him. He sat down beside Abby and handed her the tissues. She mopped up her face, blew her nose and glared at him.

"You're a terrible man, Jack Granger. You used that child to get what you want."

"You're darn right, I did." There was no repentance anywhere in his voice or in his face. "She wants the same thing I do. Why shouldn't you have to hear it from her, too?"

"But now she's all upset," Abby said.

"No, now she's watching TV." He caressed her cheek with the back of his index finger. "She's not nearly as fragile as she was, Abby. And that's because of you."

Abby batted his hand away. "Don't."

"All right." Scowling, he lowered his hand. "Then, I'll tell you I want you in my life, period. I'll use any means, fair or foul and I'll take you on any terms you name. Kitty's right, you know. We don't want just any old wife and mommy around here. We only want you."

"How can I ever believe that?"

"How can I ever believe you really want me as much as you want my daughter?" He turned sideways on the cushion to face her more fully and stretched his arm out along the top of the sofa back. "I just do, dammit. I know your heart and it's an honest heart.

Can't you believe the same about me? I've never lied to you, have I?''

Abby shook her head impatiently. ''I'm not accusing you of being dishonest, but you're still a young man. How do you know you won't change your mind about having more children later? Children of your *own.*''

''That's where your logic breaks down, honey. You love Kitty like she's your daughter. Kitty feels it, and that's why she reached out to you. I can see it. So can Millie and Erin. Can you honestly tell me you love Kitty any less because you didn't give birth to her?''

''Of course not.''

''Then, give me some credit for being able to love another child the same way. I don't have any problem with adoption. If we want more kids, we'll get them. And don't worry about that son thing. It's not an issue for me.''

''Are you sure?''

''Trust me, the Granger family name is in no danger of dying out, and even if it was, I wouldn't trade Kitty or any other daughter I had for a basketball team full of boys. My family rarely produces girls, so we think they're extra special.''

He spoke with such seriousness, she had to believe him. ''You really mean that.''

''Yes. And there's another problem with your logic.''

''What's that?''

''You want to be loved for yourself. You want me to see the real you and love you just as you are. Right?''

She nodded.

"Well, so do I. Dammit, I'm not your father. I'm not Tad the Idiot. See *me*." He thumped his chest with his fist. "See the *real* me. Not the reflections of them you're putting onto me."

"Is that what I've been doing?"

"Hell, yes," Jack said. "You've got to trust me, sweetheart. I won't be a perfect husband, but I'll give you the very best I've got to give. And I won't put impossible demands on you. We can work out the logistics of anything else, including your career."

"What do you mean?"

"I think you can accomplish your dreams living right here in Spokane. It might take you longer to get a college position, but I'll do everything I can to help you along. Or, if you really need to move, I can take the Oregon bar exam. Experienced prosecutors aren't that easy to find. Sooner or later I'll get a job down there."

Abby frowned. "But you'd have to start all over."

"Beats the hell out of losing you, Ab."

Her tears finally overflowed and ran down her cheeks. "You'd really do that for me? You love me that much?"

"Are you kidding?" He raised his hand from the back of the sofa and gently stroked her hair. "Sweetheart, I can't believe how dense you are when it comes to recognizing your own value. I'd do anything for you. I love so many things about you, I couldn't begin to list them all."

She sniffled. "Give me the top five."

Without stopping so much as a second to think, he rattled them off. "Your sense of humor, your energy and enthusiasm, your great little body and how you use it in bed, the way you like to run and you don't care about not looking perfect afterward, your intelligence, and your goals and your passion for your work. All of that is sexy as hell. Please notice that none of them has anything to do with producing children.''

"Not bad," she admitted, sniffling again. "Anything else?"

"You help me keep a balance between my home life and my work. You remind me that I'm still a man, not just a daddy or a prosecutor, that I really enjoy having a woman's company—and I'm not talking about Millie's, no offense to Millie. I'm happier when I'm around you. I have fun when I'm with you. I only hope I give you back at least half of what you give me.''

She smiled through fresh tears. "Fishing for compliments?''

"Hey." He grinned and gave her a what-can-I-say shrug. "Believe it or not, even I have some insecurities about my desirability. Kitty and I are a package deal. To a lot of women, she's nothing but baggage from a first marriage. I see it as a tremendous gift that you love her. You do love me, too, though, right?'' He frowned thoughtfully. "You know, you've never actually said the words.''

Abby took a deep breath. After the way he'd just bared his heart for her, she could hardly give him anything less than complete honesty. "Yes, Jack, I love you. I fell in love with you the first time I heard you call Kitty 'Kitten.' That's why I'm so scared of losing you later.''

"I wish I could promise that won't happen, but life doesn't give us any guarantees. What's important is that we don't waste any of the years we could have together. It's a leap of faith for both of us, Ab.'' He held out both hands to her, palms up. ''Will you take it with me?''

There was no real choice left. He was offering her the most precious things a man could give to a woman—his love, his child, his life. No matter how terrified she was of losing him, she would hate herself forever if she didn't take this risk. At its pinnacle of success, her career couldn't begin to compete with having Jack and Kitty for her family.

Fingers shaking, she reached over and touched his palms. A smile spread over his face like a brilliant sunrise. He closed his hands around hers, pulled her into his arms and kissed her with all of the longing and passion she could ever want.

Oh God, yes, this was what she wanted. She had Kitty's little handprints stamped on her heart and Jack's love engraved in her soul. No matter what the future held, life simply didn't get any better than this.

She threaded her fingers through his hair and sighed with pure pleasure when he pulled her even closer and slid his tongue into her mouth.

''*Psst.*''

The sound was too soft to really catch her attention. Then it came again, closer, louder and more insistent.

''*Psssst!*''

A laugh bubbled up inside her, but Abby went right on kissing Jack, just to see how long it took him to realize he was being paged. Kitty's next stage whisper was loud enough to penetrate a coma.

''*Psssssst! Daddy!*''

Grinning against Abby's mouth, Jack said, ''What is it?''

''What did she say?'' Kitty whispered back.

''She said yes, Kitten.''

Epilogue

Abby Granger stood outside Mountain View Elementary School, alternately glancing at her watch and scanning the road for a glimpse of Jack's car. They'd been married almost nine months now, and this was the fourth time they'd been called in for a conference with their daughter's second-grade teacher. Ah, there he was.

She waited impatiently for him to join her, but he had to stop and take off his suit coat and then his tie. He unbuttoned the top two buttons on his dress shirt as he approached her and rolled his sleeves halfway up his forearms on the way to Kitty's classroom. When he held out a hand for her to hold, she gladly took it. She'd quickly discovered that these conferences were much more nerve-racking from the parent side of the desk.

Mary Beth Dickinson greeted them with a weary

smile when they entered the room. She offered them seats at a long table. When they were all comfortably settled, Jack squeezed Abby's hand.

"Has there been any improvement?" Abby asked. "Any at all?"

"I'm afraid not," Mary Beth said. "Your daughter is the most talkative child in the entire second grade. Possibly in the entire school."

"But she's getting her work done," Jack said. "We supervise her homework every night."

"Her schoolwork's never a problem," Mary Beth said ruefully. "I wish the rest of my class learned as easily as Kitty does."

"Maybe she needs more work to do," Abby suggested. "If she was busier, she wouldn't have so much time to talk."

"Abby, I've tried that. She just whips right through everything I give her. She's already halfway through the third-grade math and almost all the way through the third-grade reading curriculum."

"What do suggest we do?" Jack asked. "Have her skip a grade?"

"It's probably going to come down to that," Mary Beth told him. "But in the meantime, will you please talk to her about being quiet in class so the other kids can learn?"

Abby nodded, though she knew it probably wouldn't do much good. It seemed as if after having been so quiet through kindergarten and first grade, Kitty was making up for lost time. Still, Abby would choose the lively, mischievous little girl who drove her teacher crazy over the quiet, sad child Kitty had been last year.

When they got up to leave, Mary Beth said, "By

the way, we'll be making Mother's Day gifts next week. Kitty seems awfully excited about that.''

"So are we," Jack told her. He turned to Abby with a knowing smile, the kind a happily married man shares with his wife. "This year, we're ready for it."

* * * * *

Feel like a star with Silhouette.

We will fly you and a guest to New York City for an exciting weekend stay at a glamorous 5-star hotel. Experience a refreshing day at one of New York's trendiest spas and have your photo taken by a professional. Plus, receive $1,000 U.S. spending money!

Flowers...long walks...dinner for two... how does Silhouette Books make romance come alive for you?

Send us a script, with 500 words or less, along with visuals (only drawings, magazine cutouts or photographs or combination thereof). Show us how Silhouette Makes Your Love Come Alive. Be creative and have fun. No purchase necessary. All entries must be clearly marked with your name, address and telephone number. All entries will become property of Silhouette and are not returnable. **Contest closes September 28, 2001.**

Please send your entry to: **Silhouette Makes You a Star!**

In U.S.A.	In Canada
P.O. Box 9069	P.O. Box 637
Buffalo, NY, 14269-9069	Fort Erie, ON, L2A 5X3

Look for contest details on the next page, by visiting www.eHarlequin.com or request a copy by sending a self-addressed envelope to the applicable address above. Contest open to Canadian and U.S. residents who are 18 or over. Void where prohibited.

Silhouette®
Where love comes alive™

Our lucky winner's photo will appear in a Silhouette ad. Join the fun!

SRMYAS1

HARLEQUIN "SILHOUETTE MAKES YOU A STAR!" CONTEST 1308
OFFICIAL RULES
NO PURCHASE NECESSARY TO ENTER

1. To enter, follow directions published in the offer to which you are responding. Contest begins June 1, 2001, and ends on September 28, 2001. Entries must be postmarked by September 28, 2001, and received by October 5, 2001. Enter by hand-printing (or typing) on an 8 ½" x 11" piece of paper your name, address (including zip code), contest number/name and attaching a script containing 500 words or less, along with drawings, photographs or magazine cutouts, or combinations thereof (i.e., collage) on no larger than 9" x 12" piece of paper, describing how the Silhouette books make romance come alive for you. Mail via first-class mail to: Harlequin "Silhouette Makes You a Star!" Contest 1308, (in the U.S.) P.O. Box 9069, Buffalo, NY 14269-9069, (in canada) P.O. Box 637, Fort Erie, Ontario, Canada L2A 5X3. Limit one entry per person, household or organization.

2. Contests will be judged by a panel of members of the Harlequin editorial, marketing and public relations staff. Fifty percent of criteria will be judged against script and fifty percent will be judged against drawing, photographs and/or magazine cutouts. Judging criteria will be based on the following:

   - Sincerity—25%
   - Originality and Creativity—50%
   - Emotionally Compelling—25%

   In the event of a tie, duplicate prizes will be awarded. Decisions of the judges are final.

3. All entries become the property of Torstar Corp. and may be used for future promotional purposes. Entries will not be returned. No responsibility is assumed for lost, late, illegible, incomplete, inaccurate, nondelivered or misdirected mail.

4. Contest open only to residents of the U.S. (except Puerto Rico) and Canada who are 18 years of age or older, and is void wherever prohibited by law; all applicable laws and regulations apply. Any litigation within the Province of Quebec respecting the conduct or organization of a publicity contest may be submitted to the Régie des alcools, des courses et des jeux for a ruling. Any litigation respecting the awarding of a prize may be submitted to the Régie des alcools, des courses et des jeux only for the purpose of helping the parties reach a settlement. Employees and immediate family members of Torstar Corp. and D. L. Blair, Inc., their affiliates, subsidiaries and all other agencies, entities and persons connected with the use, marketing or conduct of this contest are not eligible to enter. Taxes on prizes are the sole responsibility of the winner. Acceptance of any prize offered constitutes permission to use winner's name, photograph or other likeness for the purposes of advertising, trade and promotion on behalf of Torstar Corp., its affiliates and subsidiaries without further compensation to the winner, unless prohibited by law.

5. Winner will be determined no later than November 30, 2001, and will be notified by mail. Winner will be required to sign and return an Affidavit of Eligibility/Release of Liability/Publicity Release form within 15 days after winner notification. Noncompliance within that time period may result in disqualification and an alternative winner may be selected. All travelers must execute a Release of Liability prior to ticketing and must possess required travel documents (e.g., passport, photo ID) where applicable. Trip must be booked by December 31, 2001, and completed within one year of notification. No substitution of prize permitted by winner. Torstar Corp. and D. L. Blair, Inc., their parents, affiliates and subsidiaries are not responsible for errors in printing of contest, entries and/or game pieces. In the event of printing or other errors that may result in unintended prize values or duplication of prizes, all affected game pieces or entries shall be null and void. **Purchase or acceptance of a product offer does not improve your chances of winning.**

6. Prizes: (1) Grand Prize—A 2-night/3-day trip for two (2) to New York City, including round-trip coach air transportation nearest winner's home and hotel accommodations (double occupancy) at The Plaza Hotel, a glamorous afternoon makeover at a trendy New York spa, $1,000 in U.S. spending money and an opportunity to have a professional photo taken and appear in a Silhouette advertisement (approximate retail value: $7,000). (10) Ten Runner-Up Prizes of gift packages (retail value $50 ea.). Prizes consist of only those items listed as part of the prize. Limit one prize per person. Prize is valued in U.S. currency.

7. For the name of the winner (available after December 31, 2001) send a self-addressed, stamped envelope to: Harlequin "Silhouette Makes You a Star!" Contest 1197 Winners, P.O. Box 4200 Blair, NE 68009-4200 or you may access the www.eHarlequin.com Web site through February 28, 2002.

Contest sponsored by Torstar Corp., P.O Box 9042, Buffalo, NY 14269-9042.

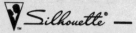

Beloved author
Sherryl Woods
is back with a brand-new miniseries

THE CALAMITY JANES

Five women. Five Dreams.
A lifetime of friendship....

On Sale May 2001–DO YOU TAKE THIS REBEL?
Silhouette Special Edition

On Sale August 2001–COURTING THE ENEMY
Silhouette Special Edition

On Sale September 2001–TO CATCH A THIEF
Silhouette Special Edition

On Sale October 2001–THE CALAMITY JANES
Silhouette Single Title

On Sale November 2001–WRANGLING THE REDHEAD
Silhouette Special Edition

"Sherryl Woods is an author who writes with
a very special warmth, wit, charm and intelligence."
—*New York Times* bestselling author
Heather Graham Pozzessere

Available at your favorite retail outlet.

Visit Silhouette at www.eHarlequin.com   SSETCJR